A Book Signing To Die For

Judy Moore

This book is a work of fiction. Names, characters, places, and incidents are the product of the author's imagination or are used fictitiously. Any resemblance to actual events or places or persons, living or dead, is entirely coincidental.

ISBN-13 979-8647475152

Mystery Novels by Judy Moore

A Book Signing to Die For

Somebody in the Neighborhood

The Mother-in-Law

Murder in Vail

Murder at the Country Club

Novellas

Pecking Order

Football Blues

Airport Christmas

The Holiday House Sitter

The Hitchhiker on Christmas Eve

Acknowledgments

Special thanks for their insights and continued support, not to mention the time they dedicated to assisting with this book, go to Jennifer Dooley, Patrick Meaney, Anne Sommers, Judy Littleton, Arlene Bailey, Bonnie Jones, Judy Witgenstein, and Allyson R. Abbott. They have no idea how much their help means to me.

Chapter One

The tiny white-haired woman stood with her hands on her hips frowning down at the college student typing on his laptop.

"You know, this isn't the public library, young man. You sit in here, you have to buy something."

The curly-haired college kid glanced up at her sheepishly and pulled down the lid of his laptop.

"Sorry," he said, quickly pushing his books into his backpack.

"This isn't the first time," the elderly woman continued, wagging her forefinger at him.

Beck O'Rourke scurried across the bookstore to join them. "Now, Grammy, Brandon usually buys a cup of coffee or a lemonade. It's not busy today, so I didn't see any harm in letting him study here."

Brandon gave her a thankful smile, but stood up and quickly left. When he opened the front door, the salty smell of sea air and a warm ocean breeze wafted inside.

Alice O'Rourke sighed at her granddaughter. "You're much too nice to ever be successful in the business world, Beck. You need to take some tips from your old grandmother."

Beck groaned. They'd had this squabble many times before. "He's just going to go somewhere else where they won't care if he doesn't buy anything."

"Fine. Let him. He can use one of their tables," her grandmother retorted.

Beck exhaled wearily. "If we're not nice to the customers, we're not going to have any."

"I am nice to the customers," her grandmother grumbled. "The ones who buy something and pay. I believe that is the definition of a customer."

"Okay, Grammy," Beck whispered in exasperation. "Just don't make a fuss in front of the other customers." She hurried back to the cash register where a tourist waited to buy a newspaper.

Beck and her grandmother owned Beach Reads bookstore together. It was a gift from Beck's widowed mother who had been swept off her feet by a wealthy

Canadian snowbird, married him, and moved to Montreal two years before. Beck grew up in the bookstore, and some of her fondest memories were of curling up in an armchair in a cozy corner of the store reading. As her mother before her, Beck adored mysteries and read every one she could get her hands on. Her mother had even named her after her favorite mystery character, *Rebecca*, by Daphne du Maurier. Not surprisingly, the shelves of the bookstore were heavily slanted toward mysteries, although they also had a wide selection of biographies, historical fiction, classics, and, of course, bestsellers.

Only a block from the Atlantic Ocean in Manatee Beach, Florida, Beach Reads wasn't just a bookstore. It was a gathering place for locals to have a cup of coffee and a muffin in the morning, or a cold drink and a sandwich on a warm afternoon. A dozen small tables with cheery seashell-print tablecloths filled half the store, and the other half contained several shelves of books and other reading materials. Armchairs and ottomans were arranged in two alcoves amongst the books, as well as in front of the bay window that looked out onto Ocean Avenue. Tourists regularly popped in to buy a paperback or a magazine for the beach, or to cool off after they'd stayed out in the sun too long.

At the back of the store stood a long counter where customers could buy scones, muffins, or Danish that Grammy brought in daily from the bakery down the block, as well as a variety of teas and coffees. Beck wished they could offer lattes and smoothies, too, but Grammy wanted nothing to do with noisy blenders in the bookstore, and Beck had to admit she was right. They kept their food and drink selections simple.

For lunch, they offered a couple of different cold gourmet sandwiches, usually tuna fish, shrimp salad, or another of Grammy's secret creations. The kitchen was Grammy's domain, and she ruled it like an iron chef. While she wasn't always easy to work with, Grammy's crusty personality was popular with locals, as well as with the snowbirds who returned to South Florida each winter. They could see right through her gruff exterior, and even if they couldn't, her famous cranberry walnut chicken salad sandwiches drew them back to the store over and over again.

On the back wall of the kitchen was a huge, colorful painting of an underwater scene with tropical fish swimming around a large loggerhead turtle. Loggerheads nested on Manatee Beach early each summer, and the babies scampered to the ocean about two months later.

The turtles were vigilantly protected by residents and had become an ever-present symbol in the seaside community. A life-size sculpture of a loggerhead stood on the sidewalk outside the bookstore.

The kitchen was also the favorite hangout of the family's pet Great Dane, a gentle giant named Coquina, whose temperament was as docile as any dog Beck had ever encountered. The huge grey dog with the doe-like eyes may have been a pussycat in personality, but her huge presence in the store made Beck and her grandmother feel safer. Coquina typically sprawled in a corner of the kitchen enjoying the aromas, lapping up any spillage, and taking frequent naps.

The last member of their South Florida family now that Beck's mother had moved to Canada with her new husband was Beck's little sister, Lizzie. Ten years younger than Beck at nineteen, Lizzie had zero interest in the family business and didn't even like to read. Her primary diversion was the boys she met on the beach where she was a lifeguard. She seemed to have a different one on her arm every week, and today was no exception. Dressed in her red lifeguard gym shorts and t-shirt, Lizzie arrived with a deeply tanned surfer boy in tow, complete with peroxided, nearly white, hair.

"Hey, Sis," Lizzie said, plopping down in a chair at a table next to the one Beck was bussing. She released her copper red hair from the clip that held it and long curly locks cascaded down her back. "Can we get a couple of lemonades?"

Beck wrinkled her brow and kept wiping the table. "You know where the drinks are, Lizzie. Get them yourself."

Lizzie's bottom lip jutted out as she sent her older sister the same mournful look she had been giving her since she was a toddler.

"C'mon, Beck! It's hot out there. I'm exhausted, and I only have a fifteen-minute break."

Beck let out a long breath and shook her head. "You heard me."

"Please, Beck," Lizzie almost whined. "You know Grammy doesn't like me going back there."

Pursing her lips, Beck turned toward her sister. "Okay, Lizzie. This time. But one of these days, you're going to have to start doing things for yourself!"

As a self-satisfied smile settled onto Lizzie's lips, Beck glanced at the young man in the bathing suit and tank top sitting across from her sister. "Can I at least get an introduction?"

Before Lizzie could respond, the boy looked up shyly and extended his hand. When he smiled, dimples appeared.

"I'm Teddy," he said. "Teddy Davis."

"Teddy's a great surfer," Lizzie beamed. "Problem is, he's distracting me from my duties. I don't want somebody to drown because I can't take my eyes off of him."

"Don't worry," Teddy responded with a self-conscious grin. "I'm a good swimmer. I can always help you out."

"Well, Teddy," Beck asked, "would you like lemonade or something else? Iced tea? A soda?"

"Water's fine, thanks." He spoke with a slight Southern accent and obviously had good manners.

Lizzie interjected, "Bring us both a lemonade, would you, Beck? I know he wants one, too. He's just too polite to ask."

Teddy started to protest, but Beck was already heading for the kitchen. As she prepared their glasses, Grammy asked curiously, "Who's the new one? I was just getting to like the old one."

Beck chuckled. "Surfer boy named Teddy."

Grammy squinted her eyes and peered at her granddaughter's latest boyfriend. "Looks like he has a few muscles in those arms. Let's get him to help us out tonight."

Tonight, Beck's favorite part of being a bookstore owner was taking place—a book signing. Beach Reads regularly hosted well-known authors who lived in the area or were passing through on a book tour to give a speech and then sign books that audience members bought from the store. Grammy loved the signings, too, because a well-known author meant a big sales day for the bookstore.

The guest author tonight was Marcia Graybill, a famous cozy mystery writer from New England. Her latest mystery had even made the *New York Times* bestseller list. Her heroine was an amateur detective who owned a bed-and-breakfast inn in a tiny hamlet in Vermont that had seen more murders than Miami during the eighties. Some of the plots were pretty farfetched, and Beck always figured out who the murderer was about halfway through, but she couldn't resist them. She'd read all but the author's latest book, which she planned to get signed that night.

When Beck returned to Lizzie's table with their lemonades, Grammy followed. So did Coquina.

"Whoa," Teddy exclaimed. "That's a big dog!"

The Great Dane walked up to Lizzie and nuzzled her for some attention.

"Her name's Coquina," Lizzie told him, as she petted the dog.

Teddy's eyes flashed a look of surprise. "That great big dog is named after that little tiny seashell?"

Beck grinned. She couldn't resist the irony when she came up with the dog's name and was thrilled when someone got it.

"Exactly!" Finally, her sister had brought home a smart one.

Lizzie rolled her eyes. "My sister has a weird sense of humor."

Lizzie directed her attention back to the dog and went into baby talk mode. "We're adorable no matter how stupid our name is, aren't we, Coquina?" Lizzie had never been crazy about her own "old fashioned" given name either, Elizabeth, another of their mother's favorite literary characters from Jane Austen's *Pride and Prejudice*.

Lizzie gave the dog a hug around the neck and a kiss on her large forehead and then took a sip of her lemonade. Beck caught her sister's eye and nodded toward their grandmother with raised eyebrows.

"Oh, uh, Teddy, this is my grandmother," Lizzie said.

"Hello, Teddy." Grammy gave him a firm handshake. "You can call me Miss Alice. Everybody else does."

She gave him a visual once-over and then said to him, "That's quite a tan you have there. I hope you're using your sunblock?"

Teddy hesitated. "Uh, probably not as much as I should."

"If you don't, you'll be very sorry when you get to be my age. Lizzie, you always have plenty of sunblock. Give some to your friend here."

"Yes, Grammy," Lizzie replied absently. She had begun to check her phone for email.

"What are you two young people doing tonight?" Grammy asked.

Lizzie's antenna immediately went up, and she eyed her grandmother suspiciously. "Why?"

"We're having a book signing and expect a pretty big crowd. It's too much for Beck to get the seats ready by herself, and I'm too old to move furniture. We'll need some extra help setting up and, then afterward, getting everything back in order." She focused a hard stare on Lizzie. "I know you'll want to pitch in, won't you, Lizzie?"

Lizzie looked like a trapped philanderer, searching for an excuse. Before she could think of one, Teddy piped up, "Sure, we'd be happy to help, Miss Alice. We don't have any plans."

The fiery gaze Lizzie sent Teddy could have scorched the earth. He squirmed uncomfortably. "Well, we don't, do we?"

Beck couldn't help chuckling. Grammy always found a way of getting what she wanted.

"Good!" Grammy said, rubbing her hands together. "The signing starts at seven o'clock, so be here promptly at six-fifteen. It should last about an hour. Then, afterward, I'll need you to get all the tables and chairs back in place for the early crowd tomorrow." With that, Grammy was off to the kitchen with Coquina at her heels.

The second she was out of hearing range, Lizzie buried her face in her hands.

"Why did you have to say that, Teddy? I hate those things. All they do is talk about books. Books, books, books. It's so boring."

Teddy shrugged. "I dunno. I was just trying to be helpful. Your grandma seemed like she really needed us."

Beck noticed a customer heading toward the cash register so she turned to leave. "And I really need the help, too," she said. "Thanks for volunteering, Teddy. And Lizzie, it won't kill you!"

Beck's choice of words may have been an omen. What she couldn't have realized was that there would be a killing that night, the first murder in Manatee Beach in over a year. And the victim would be someone at the book signing.

Chapter Two

Beck ran upstairs during a slow period about three o'clock to choose an outfit for the book signing. She always introduced the writer, and a decent-size crowd was expected tonight. So, she wanted to look nice.

The O'Rourkes lived in a three-bedroom apartment above the bookstore with a view of the ocean if you stood in just the right corner of the living room and looked between the seafood restaurant and the gift shop across the street. Beck would have much preferred to have her own apartment as she'd had when she was a college student at Florida State getting her undergraduate and master's degrees in literature. But living here with her sister and grandmother made sense with the bookstore being right downstairs, not to mention their early opening time of eight o'clock. It was so convenient, and Grammy appreciated the help, too, though the three of them butted heads on a regular basis.

Standing in front of the white rattan full-length mirror in the corner of her bedroom, Beck held up her favorite pink wrap dress in front of her. She loved the dress, especially the way it accentuated her trim waist and hit a few inches above the knee. She'd been told she had good legs, so she didn't mind showing them off a little. But Grammy had mentioned more than once that the pink color clashed with her red hair. Beck's hair wasn't nearly as bright, or striking, as Lizzie's, and she thought it was closer to strawberry blonde than to red. No one else had ever told her she shouldn't wear pink, but her grandmother's words echoed in her brain every time she wore the dress, or even thought of wearing it, as was the case today.

So, she put her favorite dress back in the closet and was debating between a yellow sundress and a more conservative long-sleeved blue one, when she heard a scream from downstairs in the bookstore. Another louder shriek followed.

Beck dashed down the stairs to find Grammy pulling Coquina away from a distraught older woman and a younger couple.

"Get that dog away from me!" screamed the overweight woman in the hibiscus print muumuu and straw hat. "It looks more like a horse than a dog."

Coquina seemed more afraid of the customer than the customer did of her and had begun to walk around nervously in circles. Beck took hold of the dog by the collar, led her back to the kitchen, and tossed her a rawhide bone to keep her occupied. Closing the gate to the kitchen behind her, Beck returned to the group where her grandmother was still apologizing.

The frightened customer with the curly greying hair sat fanning herself with her straw hat as if she were going to faint. The thirtyish woman with her, who had silky blonde hair and a tall, model-like figure, sent Beck a weary apologetic glance that spoke volumes.

"We're so sorry," the younger woman apologized. "My husband and I love dogs, but my mother-in-law is afraid of them."

Beck told them she wasn't the first customer to be afraid of the dog. "I know her appearance can be a little frightening," she said of the Great Dane, "but that's why we keep her in the store. For security reasons. Coquina has the sweetest temperament, though. She wouldn't hurt a fly."

The husband, a lanky man with wavy brown hair and glasses, nodded in agreement. “I know. Great Danes are very docile. So sorry for the commotion.” He sent an embarrassed look his mother’s way.

“Where are you folks from?” Grammy asked, picking up immediately that they were tourists.

“Up in North Carolina, the Outer Banks,” the man answered. “We get so many hurricanes up our way these days that we were thinking of moving to Florida. We’re looking around at some property while we’re down here on vacation. This seems like a nice area.”

“It’s the best,” Grammy responded, adding her oft-repeated description, “Paradise, but without the traffic. Just keep it a secret.”

The younger woman smiled. “The beach certainly is beautiful down here. We just took the nicest long walk.”

“Who knows, maybe we’ll be your neighbors one day. I’m Joe Davidson,” the man said, reaching out to shake hands with Grammy. He had a polite, genteel way about him. “This is my wife, Lisa, and my mother, Peggy Davidson.”

Beck introduced herself and her grandmother and asked them if she could help them with anything.

The young couple glanced at the seated older woman who still seemed flustered from her encounter with the dog. She glanced up and realized they were waiting for her to speak.

"Oh, yes, well, I just noticed the sign in your window about the book signing tonight and thought I might like to come. But now I'm not so sure." She knitted her eyebrows into a frown. "Will that animal be here?"

Beck's eyes widened and she bit her lip. She didn't like the way the woman was talking about her beloved Coquina. Trying not to take offense, she reminded herself that not everyone was a dog lover.

"No, we put her away when we have an event," Beck told her. "You have nothing to worry about." They kept Coquina upstairs during book signings, not so much for the guests' sake, but because the Great Dane became nervous in large groups of people.

Peggy Davidson didn't seem convinced. "Well, if you're sure that dog won't be here."

"No, no," Grammy assured her. "Coquina definitely will not be here."

Mrs. Davidson appeared somewhat mollified. "Well, all right then. I do enjoy Marcia Graybill's books, and I'd like the chance to see her."

The woman glanced at the photo of Marcia Graybill on the poster on the wall. "She looks so familiar to me. I think I may know her. I went to high school with a girl named Marcia Cox who looks just like her."

Grammy's eyes twinkled. "Wouldn't that be something? You two could have a little high school reunion."

"I didn't know her too well," the woman said, "but I do remember her name and her face. I'm not sure why. My memory isn't what it used to be."

"Well," Grammy said, shifting into sales mode, "we have several of her different books for sale that she will be happy to autograph for you. You might even want to get some for your old high school friends back in North Carolina, too. Wouldn't that be a nice gift?"

"It would be nice to have my own autographed copy," Peggy said, brightening.

"Well, you must come then," Beck encouraged her.

Beck wanted as large a crowd as possible for the well-known mystery author. She'd had to coax the publisher to include Beach Reads on the tour, so she wanted to be sure the event was well attended. It could mean more top-name authors in the future.

"All right," the woman agreed with an uneasy smile. "I'll try to come then. What time does it start again?"

"It begins at seven, but you may want to arrive a few minutes early to get a good seat," Beck suggested. "We're expecting quite a few people."

Grammy eyed the younger couple. "And will you both be coming as well?" Beck could almost see the dollar signs register in her grandmother's eyes.

"Oh, no, no," the daughter-in-law answered quickly. Beck suspected she was looking forward to a break from her husband's mother. "Joe and I may have a date night tonight. There's a restaurant down the street we wanted to try. Right, Joe?"

Her husband nodded, but asked his mother with a note of concern, "If you're sure you'll be okay on your own?"

His mother nodded her approval. "Oh, of course. The hotel's right down the block. I'll be fine. You two go out and have a nice dinner."

Beck happened to glance down at the seated woman's hand and noticed the largest emerald stone she'd ever seen.

"Wow!" she blurted without thinking. "What a gorgeous ring."

Obviously pleased, Peggy held out her hand so they could take a closer look at the circular stone that was about the size of a quarter. "A gift from my late husband, may he rest in peace. For our thirty-fifth wedding anniversary."

Grammy took hold of her hand. "Well, he certainly had good taste. That's about the prettiest ring I've ever seen."

After a few more minutes of small talk, they said goodbye and left the store. Beck was pleased she'd been able to recruit another audience member for that night's book signing.

Chapter Three

Lizzie and Teddy reported for duty as directed, right on time at six-fifteen. But Lizzie wasn't happy about it. She sulked the entire time as she and Teddy set up about forty chairs, as well as a dais with a microphone and a table where the author could sign her books. The chairs were arranged with their backs to the bookshelves and the kitchen and cash register to the left of the audience.

Beck had stacked dozens of the author's various books on a table next to the cash register, ready for Grammy to ring up sales. Grammy was busy in the kitchen baking brownies and brewing coffee for the guests. Naturally, she would have preferred to sell drinks and snacks to the people attending, but Beck had convinced her long ago that their events would be nicer and better attended if some snacks were complimentary.

Beck had decided on the yellow sundress and was giving her makeup one final check when Lizzie came bounding up the stairs.

"Beck, can Teddy and I go now?" she asked, out of breath. "Everything's all set up the way Grammy told us. I don't want to have to sit through the book thing and neither does Teddy. We wanna go get a burger at Kerrigan's."

Beck shrugged. "Fine with me if everything's done. Just be back here about eight, okay? We want everything cleaned up and ready for tomorrow morning. Grammy and I will be bushed afterward and don't want to be up cleaning all night."

"I promise," Lizzie said, already half-way down the stairs. "You tell Grammy."

Beck had been running interference for Lizzie with Grammy for as long as she could remember. Lizzie loved her grandmother to death, but she found her intimidating and tried to avoid her anytime she thought Grammy might disapprove.

"And, Lizzie," Beck called down after her.

Lizzie skidded to a stop and turned around.

"Thanks for helping. I really needed it."

Lizzie grinned. "No prob. What are sisters for?" Then Lizzie did something totally unexpected. She skipped back up the stairs, gave her sister a tight hug, and was gone before Beck had time to react.

Still enjoying the moment, Beck ran a comb through her shoulder-length hair one more time and added a little more mascara to her thick eyelashes, really accentuating her green eyes. Giving her reflection a self-appraising look, she said to herself, "I guess I'm as ready as I'll ever be."

She glanced over her note cards one more time. Public speaking wasn't her favorite thing. No, that was an understatement. She absolutely abhorred speaking in front of an audience, and for good reason. But as she'd gotten older, her nerves had settled, and she'd gained more confidence in her public speaking ability. Beforehand, she always practiced with her note cards in front of the mirror until she felt she was totally ready. After introducing so many authors over the past few years, she'd begun to get used to it and felt much more comfortable than she had when she first started. Some of the authors, especially the really famous ones, she found a little intimidating. But she felt much more comfortable with cozy mystery writers who were usually so sweet and down-to-earth.

When she went downstairs, the delicious aroma of baked brownies and freshly brewed coffee filled the room. Gazing around the bookstore, she was taken with how warm and appealing their little store had become. They'd worked so hard to make it a homey and comfortable refuge for tourists and town residents to get out of the glare of the bright Florida sunshine and relax for a while in their little literary world.

The author was supposed to arrive fifteen minutes ahead of time, and Beck just hoped she wouldn't be late. That had happened once or twice in the past, and it had been incredibly awkward, to say the least, having to stall in front of the audience. When the front door swung open, Beck glanced over quickly, hoping to see Marcia Graybill, the author. But it was Grammy's friend, Dorothy, pushing a baby carriage. Beck knew there was no baby in that carriage, but Dorothy's aging white poodle, Fifi. Anywhere Dorothy went, Fifi went with her. Shutting the door behind her, the elderly woman pushed the carriage into a corner of the room and reached down to pick up the poodle.

"Hello, Dorothy," Grammy called out to her from the kitchen. "I'm glad you could make it."

"Wouldn't have missed it," Dorothy replied, crossing the room. "This is one author you're having whose books I've actually read!"

When she saw the plateful of brownies neatly stacked on the snack bar, Dorothy reached out a wrinkled, suntanned arm to take one.

Grammy slapped her hand. "Not yet, Dorothy. You're messing up my arrangement. Wait 'til everybody gets here."

Dorothy shrugged and glanced around the kitchen. "Where's Coquina? Fifi wants to play." Dorothy set the little dog down, and the poodle immediately began sniffing the kitchen floor for any morsels she could find.

"We had to put her upstairs," Grammy said, not looking up from the sink where she had begun rinsing out the brownie pan. "A tourist who's coming is afraid of her. Doesn't like dogs."

Dorothy looked shocked. "Doesn't like dogs? What's wrong with her?"

Grammy shrugged. "You know how some people are. She'll probably be afraid of Fifi, too."

Dorothy frowned in disbelief. "Afraid of my Fifi? Who'd be afraid of my sweet little Fifi?"

"The way that lady tourist screamed today, it wouldn't surprise me at all if she would be," Grammy answered, drying her hands with a dish towel. "Why don't we take Fifi upstairs and let her stay with Coquina during the signing?"

As the two elderly women climbed the stairs, coaxing the poodle behind them, the front door swung open again and Beck looked up eagerly, hoping to see the author. Instead, it was the owners of the jewelry store next door, two of her least favorite people, Phil and Lydia Merritt. They always complained about Beach Reads' customers taking all the parking spaces. Concerned, Beck hurried over to them.

"I know you close at six, so I didn't think parking would be a problem tonight," Beck began.

Lydia Merritt interrupted. "No, no. We're not here about that, although earlier in the day there wasn't a spot to be found, and one of our best customers had to park over a block away." The fiftyish woman pursed her lips and smoothed her frosted hair, which she always wore pulled back in a tight bun. "Actually, Marcia Graybill is one of my favorite authors."

Beck let out a sigh of relief. The last thing she needed tonight was another debate about the limited parking in front of their stores.

"Oh, wonderful, Lydia. I'm so glad you came. Are you a fan too, Phil?"

Phil, a tall, balding man who was the quiet one of the couple, shook his head. "Me? Oh no. Just here with Lydia."

The Merritts were one of those couples, Beck noticed, who did everything together. Everything. She'd never seen one without the other. Being single and as independent as she was, Beck found that difficult to understand. But it obviously worked for some couples, so who was she to judge?

"Please, help yourself to some coffee and a brownie," she offered, guiding them toward the kitchen counter. The door opened again and several more customers entered, but no Marcia Graybill. Beck glanced at her watch. She was beginning to get a little nervous. The author should have been here by now.

Phil picked up a brownie and just as he took a big bite, Grammy appeared on the staircase. She stopped in her tracks and glared at him. Beck saw the look in her grandmother's eyes and quickly interceded.

"Grammy," Beck said slowly, hoping to dispel any animosity her grandmother might feel, "Phil and Lydia from next door decided to come tonight. Marcia Graybill is one of Lydia's favorite authors. Isn't that nice?"

"I know Lydia and Phil are from next-door," Grammy growled at Beck. Then she asked them bluntly, "Y'all aren't here to complain about the parking, are you?"

"Not this time," Lydia responded, appearing to prepare herself for battle. "Though today, one of our best customers had to park over a block away during your lunch hour."

"Exercise probably did her good," Grammy muttered, as she descended the staircase and went behind the counter.

Her friend Dorothy followed behind her and eyed Phil eating the brownie. "How come he gets to have a brownie and I couldn't?"

Phil stopped mid-bite. "Oh, I'm sorry, Miss Alice. I thought the brownies were for the customers."

Beck stepped in. She could feel trouble brewing. "Of course, the brownies are for the customers, Phil. Help yourself." She walked behind the counter. "Can I offer you both a cup of coffee?"

Beck could see Grammy's ill-tempered feathers were ruffled and wasn't surprised when her grandmother asked, "How many of the author's books would you like to buy, Lydia? We have all ten of them available. How about one of each?"

Lydia seemed unfazed. "Oh, I don't need to buy one. I brought my own from home for her to sign." She pulled a worn paperback out of her purse and showed it to Grammy.

Grammy narrowed her sharp blue eyes at her next-door neighbor. "I don't come in your store and–"

Beck cut her off when she heard a commotion at the front door. Relieved, she exclaimed, "Oh, look! Here's Marcia Graybill now."

Chapter Four

Marcia Graybill entered the store with a flourish. She wore a teal blue cape that she unfurled like a matador exposing a matching knee-length sheath dress beneath. Several customers entering the store at the same time squealed in admiration. Beck sensed she wasn't really late, but rather just liked making an entrance.

The author gave her fans a little wave and handed the cape along with her handbag to her white-haired, mustachioed husband, who looked like he'd been through the scenario many times before. Her shiny blonde hair was teased and hair-sprayed to perfection, and her bright red lipstick shone like a ripe tomato across the entire room. Beck knew from reading background information on the author that she was sixty-five years old, but she appeared much younger.

Beck approached the guest of honor to welcome her and lead her to the back office where she would wait out of sight of the audience to be introduced.

"I'm Beck O'Rourke, owner of Beach Reads," she informed the author, extending her hand. She received the limpest of handshakes in return. "We're thrilled to have you with us tonight. I'm a big fan."

"Yes, of course, dear, of course," the author answered, as she glanced around the bookstore in a noncommittal way as they walked together across the room to the back office. Beck couldn't tell if she liked what she saw or not. "Rather a small store, isn't it?" was all that she said.

Beck ignored the comment and invited her to take a seat on the only chair in the bookstore's tiny office. "Could I get you a cup of coffee, Ms. Graybill? Or may I call you Marcia?"

"No, no. Ms. Graybill is fine. No coffee. I don't suppose I could get a martini, could I?"

Both answers took Beck by surprise. She'd never met a cozy mystery author who was quite so—flamboyant, she guessed was the word.

"No, I'm sorry, Ms. Graybill. We don't have a liquor license here. But I could get you a soda or lemonade if you'd like."

The author wrinkled her nose. "Just sparkling water then. You can manage that, can't you?"

Beck wasn't sure she could. They had bottled water, but not sparkling water. The author saw her hesitate.

"Oh, never mind then, never mind." Her tone was incredulous. "I'll get something afterward at the hotel up the street. I guess that rattrap passes for a hotel around here."

"You mean the Manatee Beach Hotel?" Beck asked, not hiding her surprise. She couldn't believe the woman was disparaging the best hotel for miles around. It wasn't that large, but it had a wonderful Key West-style ambiance about it, all the modern amenities, as well as a four-star oceanside restaurant. And every room had a direct ocean view.

When the woman nodded, Beck couldn't help joking with her, not making much attempt to hide her sarcasm, "Not up to the standards of the Wildflower Inn, I guess?"

For the first time, the author gave a flicker of a smile at the mention of the literary setting of her mystery books, and Beck released a sigh of relief that she'd broken a small sliver of ice with this cold author. Beck realized the woman was one of the most popular mystery authors in the country right now, but still. Many better-known authors who had spoken at Beach Reads were much more gracious.

"I'll be introducing you," Beck said. "Is there anything in particular you'd like for me to say?"

The coldness came back immediately. "You received my bio, I presume?"

"Yes, of course. I just thought—"

She waved her hand dismissively. "That's fine."

Beck checked her watch. Two minutes until seven. They liked to start on time, but she wanted to be sure most of the seats were filled. Peeking out the door, Beck saw that only a couple of seats were empty, and some people were standing in the back.

Grammy stood behind the cash register, in her element, selling books. Five or six people were waiting in line, but Grammy took her time with each one of them, trying to upsell as many copies as she could. She'd definitely missed her calling. If she'd started when she was young, her grandmother could have made a killing as a Wall Street stockbroker.

Gazing across the audience, Beck noticed the woman from that afternoon, the one who was afraid of the dog, front and center. She looked so much nicer than she did earlier in the day, when she stopped in after walking on the beach. Her brownish-grey hair was styled beautifully, and she wore an attractive blue pants suit. Seated next to her were the jewelry store owners from next door, Lydia and Phil Merritt, and on the other side was Grammy's friend, Dorothy.

As Beck glanced around the room, she recognized several familiar faces from around town, many of whom were regular customers—a florist from down the block, the local librarian, two real estate agents. And there were a number of new faces, too, tourists, she assumed, who were interested in seeing the famous author.

Beck turned her attention back to Marcia Graybill, who sat in Beck's office chair, nervously jiggling her foot.

"Let's wait another few minutes," Beck told the author. "Some people are still buying your books."

"Well, that's good news anyway," Ms. Graybill sniffed as she crossed, and then recrossed, her legs in the office chair.

The woman seemed edgy and uncomfortable. “Hey, hon,” she asked Beck, “would you mind going out there and getting my purse from my husband? I need a cigarette.”

Beck grimaced and drew in her breath. She knew the author wouldn’t be pleased with what she had to say. “I’m sorry, Ms. Graybill, but smoking isn’t allowed in the store.”

Marcia Graybill stared at the ceiling in seeming disbelief. “Just a puff or two. It relaxes me before I go on.”

“I’d love to help you, Ms. Graybill, but it’s state law. No smoking in retail establishments.”

The author’s eyebrows knitted together and she peered around. “Isn’t there a back door or something where I can step outside?”

Beck shook her head. “The only back door is through the kitchen and everyone will see you if you go out that way.”

“Oh, for God’s sake! What kind of a two-bit—”

Beck could feel her Irish temper rising. Her face reddened, and she turned away from the woman to peek out the door, hoping the line was shorter at the cash register. If she didn’t get away from Marcia Graybill soon, Beck knew she'd say something she'd regret and that could mean an end to future book signings for the store.

Only one person was left at the cash register, so Beck decided it was time to start. Picking up her note cards, she turned to the author and told her, "All right. I'm going out to introduce you now. You should be able to hear me. When the audience applauds, come on out and go to the dais with the microphone."

Marcia Graybill rolled her eyes at Beck and waved her away.

"I wasn't born yesterday, hon. I know the drill."

Chapter Five

Beck stood for a moment to the side of the front row, waiting for Grammy to finish her sale. Two chairs away, she heard Lydia Merritt making polite conversation with the tourist seated next to her when she happened to look down and notice her emerald ring.

"My goodness," the jewelry store owner gushed to Peggy Davidson. "In all my years of dealing with gems, I don't think I've ever seen such a large and high-quality emerald. It's absolutely breathtaking."

Peggy proudly held out her hand and explained that it had been a gift from her now-departed husband on the occasion of their thirty-fifth anniversary.

Lydia elbowed her husband. "Phil, look at this emerald."

Phil, glancing politely at first, took a double take when he saw the size of the ring.

"My God!" he exclaimed, taking the tourist's hand. "It's exquisite."

Grammy's friend Dorothy, seated on the other side of Peggy, craned her neck to get a look at the ring. "Let me see. I want to see it, too."

Peggy turned toward the elderly woman and extended her hand. The woman on the other side of Dorothy, a real estate agent named Lucy, peered at the ring, too.

"Lordy, Lordy," Dorothy exclaimed. "That is some rock!"

Beck couldn't help but smile at Dorothy's comment. Glancing over at the cash register, she saw that her grandmother had finished her sale. It was time to start. She took a deep breath, walked to the dais, and waited for the audience to quiet down.

"Welcome to Beach Reads, everyone," she said into the microphone, flashing a big smile to a smattering of applause. She guessed there were about fifty people in the room. Feeling her face flush, she bit her lip and tried to calm her nerves.

"Thank you so much for coming to hear one of the nation's most popular mystery authors, Marcia Graybill. Ms. Graybill's cozy mystery series set at the Wildflowers bed-and-breakfast inn in Vermont is currently the number one best-selling cozy mystery in the country. So, we feel very fortunate to have her with us."

The crowd murmured at that revelation, and Beck continued with an enthusiasm she didn't feel. Any admiration she'd ever felt for the author had gone down the drain after spending five minutes in her company.

"If you're not familiar with what a cozy mystery is, it's kind of a Hallmark version of a mystery—no swearing, no extreme violence, and definitely G-rated. They're very popular nowadays. Cozy mysteries are typically set in a small town in a cozy environment, like a cafe, a quilting shop, or, in this case, a bed-and-breakfast inn. And they typically have an amateur sleuth who solves the crimes.

"I know I've been a big fan of Marcia Graybill's books since I read her first one ten years ago, *The Dead and Breakfast Inn*. I'm sure many of you have read that one, too." A few women in the audience nodded.

"And I can't wait to read her latest book, *Hotcakes and Homicide,* featuring her fearless sleuth, Annabelle James."

Beck paused to catch her grandmother's eye in the crowd. "If you don't have your copy yet for Ms. Graybill to personally autograph after her presentation, I'm sure my grandmother, Miss Alice, will be more than happy to sell you one."

Standing near the cash register, Grammy waved to the crowd. "I most certainly will," she announced enthusiastically. "And don't forget we have all nine of her other books as well." She picked up a few to show the audience, pushing her product as well as any carnival barker. "*Coffee, Croissants, and Corpses; Maid for Murder; Antiques and Arsenic.* You don't want to miss your chance to have them personally autographed by the author."

A few people in the crowd chuckled. They weren't strangers to Grammy's hard-sell tactics.

"After Ms. Graybill speaks," Beck continued, "we'll have a short question-and-answer period. Then, if you'll form a line to your right, each one of you can personally talk to the author, have your book signed, and even get a photo with her if you brought your cell phone. Speaking of phones, would everyone please check to be sure they are silenced during Ms. Graybill's speech."

The crowd murmured again, and Beck heard Dorothy in the front row complain that she'd forgotten her cell phone.

"Without any further ado, please join me in welcoming Beach Reads' featured author, Marcia Graybill." Beck began applauding as she stepped to the side of the room and the audience followed suit.

Marcia Graybill floated into the room, blowing kisses and gushing at the applause as she approached the microphone.

"Oh, you are all too kind!" she told them sweetly as they continued to applaud. "All this for little ole me? My goodness. What a wonderful audience you are!"

Beck stood stone-faced in the back of the room, leaning against the wall with her arms crossed, trying to reconcile this friendly, warmhearted woman with the nasty, arrogant one she'd been talking to earlier.

"I feel so fortunate to be here with you in your lovely little town," the author chirped in the sweetest of voices to the audience. "And what a nice surprise to have all this beautiful sunshine and warm weather in the month of March. Why the day I left back home, it was snowing!"

Audience members nodded and seemed to be congratulating themselves for having the good sense to live in a place that was warm all year round.

"Not that I'd ever consider leaving my dear, dear New England, mind you. Such a quaint, picturesque place. Have any of you ever been up Vermont way?"

About half of the audience members raised their hands. "Then you know what I'm talking about," she said, exuding charm that Beck wouldn't have believed she possessed. "And the rest of you really must come visit someday soon so you can get a better picture of where my Wildwood Inn is set. You must!"

A tanned hand with dirty fingernails went up in the middle of the second row, and Beck was dismayed to see that it belonged to Scratchoff McLean. Scratchoff, a self-proclaimed beach bum who had been homeless for years, won the state's scratch-off lottery the year before for one million dollars. Admirably, he'd used his winnings to buy a small, deserted motel where he and others who didn't have homes could live. It was a few blocks away from the bookstore. He was undoubtedly Manatee Beach's most colorful character and, since his lottery win, spent his days riding his beach bike around town as a self-appointed welcoming committee, gregariously visiting with tourists and residents alike.

When a surprised Marcia Graybill glanced his way, he stood up. “Er, uh, Mrs., uh, writer lady,” he said, running his hand through his stringy blond hair.

“Graybill,” the author answered in a considerably less friendly tone than she’d been speaking in previously. “I’ll be taking quest—”

“Yeah, Mrs. Graybill, ma’am. I’d be mighty interested in what you was just sayin’ about goin’ up there to Vermont. I come into some money recently, ya see, and I’m hopin’ to do some travelin’ around a little bit. ‘Bout how much would you say it costs to stay in that there Wildflower Inn?”

Several members of the audience tittered at his question.

“Well, sir,” the author answered, obviously trying to suppress a laugh, “the Wildflower Inn isn’t actually a real place. It’s fictional.”

“Not real? You mean make-believe? How can I stay in a make-believe hotel?”

Beck groaned. Marcia Graybill had looked down her nose enough at their town before Scratchoff made them all look like fools.

Grammy piped up. She never took much lip from Scratchoff.

"Scratchoff, you go on and sit down now and let this lady talk. She's gonna take questions later—questions that make sense!"

"Now, Miss Alice, there ain't no need—"

"You heard me, Scratchoff. Go on now. Sit down and be quiet!"

Looking like she'd hurt his feelings, Scratchoff begrudgingly took his seat. Grammy nodded at Ms. Graybill. "You can go ahead now."

The author seemed thrown off track for a moment, but she quickly recovered. She told them she hadn't started writing until after her children were grown and about how she'd struggled to get published. She encouraged audience members to follow their dreams, no matter their age, no matter the obstacles, which impressed Beck. Maybe this woman wasn't as arrogant and self-serving as she had thought.

And Beck really felt she might have misjudged the author when she began to relate the difficult childhood she'd had growing up in a poor family in North Carolina and some of the challenges she'd had to overcome.

For the second time that evening, an audience member abruptly interrupted Ms. Graybill's speech.

"I knew you looked familiar!" Peggy Davidson exclaimed from the front row. "We went to high school together. I'm Peggy. Remember me? I was Peggy Pope back then. And you were Marcia Cox."

Marcia Graybill was taken aback, and probably a little embarrassed, too, because the tourist who was afraid of dogs looked a good twenty years older than she did. The author certainly didn't appear pleased about seeing her old classmate, but she tried to cover as best she could. "Well, what do you know? Isn't it a small world?"

The author brushed past the incident, but it seemed to upset her, and she ended her talk soon afterward. In the question-and-answer session, several people asked questions about her writing routine, her upcoming projects, and other authors who had influenced her. Standing next to Beck, still holding his wife's cape and purse, the author's husband kept tapping his watch, obviously trying to signal his wife that it was time to wrap it up. Must be getting anxious for martini time, Beck figured.

Beck took the hint, though, and stepped to the front of the room to tell the audience that there was time for only one more question. Scratchoff's hand was waving wildly in the air, but Beck ignored him and called on the local librarian who asked an intelligent question about character development. A good note to end on.

Beck thanked the author, led the applause, and announced that the book signing would begin immediately.

Chapter Six

Not everyone wanted to have a book signed, and some left the store right after the talk ended. Others made their way to the snack bar to help themselves to a cup of coffee and a brownie. Marcia Graybill took a quick break to talk to her husband, while about thirty mystery fans lined up with their newly purchased books to be signed. Grammy went down the row of customers with a post-it note pad and asked each one for the correct spelling of the name they would like the author to inscribe. Some people had multiple books to be signed, and Grammy placed a post-it note with the requested name on each title page to be autographed.

Beck helped the author get settled in at the table and ushered the first person in line to the author—the jewelry store owner from next door, Lydia Merritt. She produced her well-worn copy of *The Dead and Breakfast Inn* for the author's signature. Marcia Graybill pursed her lips and gave Beck a withering sideways glance. She clearly wasn't pleased to be signing an old book. The point of these book signings was to sell more new books.

"I've been a fan for such a long time," Lydia gushed. "I can't believe I'm actually getting to meet you in person!"

Ms. Graybill gave her a half-smile as she signed the book. "Well, thank you, dear."

Lydia took her cell phone from her purse and handed it to Beck. "Where should I stand for my picture?"

The author frowned and motioned to Beck. She whispered, "I don't want to have my picture taken with all these people. It will take much too long."

Beck wasn't about to allow a photo op to be taken away from her customers. Especially not after she'd promised them they could have one. Taking Ms. Graybill by the arm, she pulled her to the side, out of hearing distance of the customers.

"Now, Ms. Graybill," she began, "I know you're anxious to get out of here to go have a cigarette and probably a drink, too."

The author gaped at her, clearly affronted. She wasn't used to being spoken to that way.

"How dare—"

Beck continued, undeterred, playing to the woman's ego. "I know posing for a picture with your fans may not mean much to you, but you have to remember that it means everything to them. Many of them will place the photo in their living rooms and boast about meeting you to their friends. To them, this is one of the most memorable nights of their lives. I know you don't want to take that away from them."

She knew she'd laid it on a little thick, but the message seemed to have gotten through. Ms. Graybill appeared to give it some serious thought. Then she lifted her chin, straightened her back, and declared to Beck, "You know, dear, you are absolutely right. I owe this to my fans."

She stepped away, walked around the table, and put her arm around Lydia Merritt's waist. Beck had never seen sourpuss Lydia look that elated before. As Beck snapped away, Marcia Graybill couldn't have been more gracious.

Dorothy was next in line and spent a little too much time telling the author about her poodle, Fifi. But Ms.

Graybill took it in stride and even added Fifi's name to the inscription, which thrilled Dorothy no end. Since Dorothy had forgotten her phone, Beck took a photo of her with the author on her own phone and promised to email it to her.

Peggy, the dog-hater, was next, and Beck could see that she made Marcia Graybill uncomfortable. When she again brought up that they had been high school classmates, the author barely acknowledged her as she signed the book.

It was apparent Peggy wanted to talk more but, because of the long line, she suggested she would wait until the book signing had ended so they could "catch up." The author smiled noncommittally as they posed for a picture together.

Beck repeated the routine for a few more customers when she heard the front door open and saw out of the corner of her eye Lizzie and Teddy coming into the store. It must be eight o'clock already, she said to herself. The night had gone quickly. As Grammy tasked Lizzie and Teddy with starting to get the chairs moved back into their regular positions and tidying up the kitchen area, Beck continued the slow process of ushering each fan to the table for their book signing and photo.

Ms. Graybill had apparently taken Beck's comments to heart because she was spending extended time with each of her fans, which Beck found impossible to believe was typically the case. In fact, this book signing was taking longer than any of the previous ones Beach Reads had ever hosted.

When she glanced around the room between customers, Beck noticed Peggy Davidson in a lengthy conversation with the author's husband near the cash register. The next time Beck looked around the room, at least fifteen minutes later, the author's weary-looking husband was sitting down, checking his watch again. She didn't see Peggy Davidson anywhere and figured she must have gotten tired of waiting to talk to her old classmate and left.

Finally, at about eight forty-five, Beck snapped a picture of the final customer in line with Ms. Graybill and approached the author.

"I hope you don't mind one more autograph," Beck said with a bright smile, handing her a new copy of *Hotcakes and Homicide*. "I've been a fan of your books for a long time."

Mrs. Graybill looked up at her with a tired smile as she took the book. “Of course, dear. And thank you so much for your assistance tonight.”

The author took longer signing the book than Beck expected.

“I hope you were pleased with the turnout tonight?” Beck asked when she finished writing.

The author was gracious in her reply and sounded surprisingly sincere. “Very much so. It was a very well-run event.”

Beck was thrilled with the comment. “Well, thank you very much. That means a lot coming from you.”

Marcia Graybill smiled and handed Beck the book. “Well,” she said with a weary sigh, “I think it’s time for that drink and a cigarette.”

Beck felt her face flush. “Oh, I didn’t mean—”

The author laughed. “Never you mind, dear. I’m just joking with you.” Then she did something very unexpected. She leaned forward and gave Beck a hug.

“Thank you very much … for everything.”

As Beck watched the author take her husband’s arm and leave the store, she flipped open the cover of the book and read the inscription. *“Beck, Thank you for reminding me what's really important. I won't forget it. All the best always, Marcia Graybill."*

Chapter Seven

When Beck approached the snack counter, Lizzie and Teddy were sitting on stools next to each other sipping sodas. Grammy was tidying up the kitchen, and the only customer left in the store was Scratchoff, who had one brownie in his mouth and another one wrapped in a napkin that he was stuffing into his pocket. Beck knew he was waiting to ask for the leftovers to take back to the motel for the homeless people who stayed there. As usual, she was happy to help. Sometimes she'd slip in other pastries or sandwiches that she thought the residents might enjoy.

"Whew!" Beck said as she sat down on the stool next to Lizzie. "I'm exhausted, but I thought it went well. How were sales, Grammy?"

"The best we've had all year. Cha-ching!" Grammy replied cheerily, pouring a cup of coffee for her granddaughter. "One lady bought all ten of her books!"

Beck was thrilled to hear that. "That's fantastic! I thought the crowd was bigger than normal." She glanced at her sister and her boyfriend. "And thank you both for helping. You did a great job."

Lizzie smiled at her sweetly, and Teddy said, "No problem."

Scratchoff, who was leaning against the far end of the snack bar, said to Beck. "It was a right nice evenin', Miss Beck. I think I even learned a thing or two."

Grammy stopped wiping the counter and turned her critical eye on him. "What did you learn, Scratchoff? That you can't go on vacation to a fictional place?"

Lizzie giggled and leaned forward to peer down the snack bar at Scratchoff.

"Now, Miss Alice, there was no call for you to go off on me like that in front of all them people."

Lizzie laughed and whispered to Teddy in a voice loud enough for Beck to hear, "Wish I'd seen that!"

Grammy's lips tightened into a firm line. "It was bad enough to ask such a ridiculous question, making all of us look like a bunch of hicks in front of that famous author," she scolded. "But besides that, Scratchoff, Beck told everybody there'd be a question-and-answer period at the end. The lady had barely started talking before you interrupted her."

A sheepish look flashed across Scratchoff's face. "Well, I'm sorry if I embarrassed y'all. I guess I still have a lot to learn about all the social nicety nices. But I'm tryin'. Ever since I won all that money I been tryin' real hard to be a upstandin' citizen. Guess I'm gonna slip up sometimes."

"Well, try harder," Grammy admonished him. "Especially when you're in our store."

Lizzie laughed and Scratchoff turned to her and Teddy, looking like he needed to explain himself. "Ya see, when I was a young'un like you there," he said, nodding at Teddy, "I didn't have no ambition. Not one little bit. All I wanted to do was surf and hang out with my friends. Trouble is, I never grew out of it. Been a beach bum my whole life."

He eyed Teddy's light blond hair and tanned skin. "Even looked a little like you back then. Don't you go down the wrong path, young man. You get yourself some ambition."

"I've got ambition," Teddy responded. "I'm enrolling in college this fall. I'm gonna study business."

"Well, good for you." Scratchoff sounded impressed. Then he turned his attention to Lizzie. "And what about you, young lady? Have you got some ambition?"

She shrugged. "I don't know. Right now, I'm just happy being a lifeguard."

Beck interjected. "Lizzie will be going to college soon, isn't that right, Grammy? She's just taking a little time off now after high school."

"Darn right," Grammy said, staring Lizzie in the eye. "And the sooner the better. Don't want to wait too long or you'll get out of the studying habit."

"Ugh," Lizzie groaned, stepping down from the barstool. "Will you two get off my back? I'll go to college when I'm good and ready." She tapped Teddy on the arm. "C'mon, Teddy. Let's go watch TV."

They climbed the stairs to the apartment living room, leaving only Scratchoff in the store. He walked over to Beck.

"Since everbody's gone, you reckon I can take the rest of them brownies back to the folks at the motel?" he asked.

"Of course, you can," Beck answered, standing up to find an aluminum tin for the brownies. "Grammy, anything else we can send over to the homeless people at the motel?"

Her grandmother gave Scratchoff an unexpected little smile. "I guess I was a little hard on you tonight, so why don't you go ahead and take these leftover sandwiches and muffins. Here's a jug of iced tea, too. I made too much today."

Scratchoff's face lit up. "I knowed beneath all that huff and puff there beat a heart of gold. I sure did. Thank you, Miss Alice."

Grammy ignored the compliment, handed him the food, and shooed him out of the store. Beck walked outside with him and helped him load the food containers into the large wire basket on the front of his blue beach bike. As she watched him take off pedaling down the street, she noticed the souvenir shop across the street had already closed and realized it must be after nine o'clock. All the other stores on Ocean Avenue closed at six. It was the only one that stayed open late.

Locking the front door and closing the blinds, Beck helped her grandmother finish tidying up the kitchen and then went to the office where she spent the next hour tallying sales, placing orders, and doing other bookwork. She had just turned off the lights when she heard a loud knock on the front door.

Peeking through the blinds, Beck recognized a young couple she'd met earlier that day. She couldn't remember their names.

"Sorry, we're closed," she said, through the half-opened door.

"Closed?" the man asked, wrinkling his brow. "Then my mother's not still there? At the book signing?"

"Oh, no. The book signing ended over an hour ago."

The man appeared visibly upset. "We're looking for my mother and can't find her anywhere," he said. "I don't know if you remember us from this afternoon. My mother is Peggy Davidson. I'm her son, Joe, and this is my wife, Lisa. My mother was the one who got upset about your dog."

"Oh yes, of course, I remember your mother," Beck said, moving back from the door and flipping on the light. "Please step inside."

The distressed man and his wife entered the store. "My mother was supposed to meet us back at the hotel after the book signing, but she never showed up. We've looked everywhere, but we can't find her. Did you see her at the book signing?"

"Oh, yes," Beck answered. "She was sitting right in the front row and then had her book signed afterward."

Worry lines wrinkled the man's forehead. "I don't understand where she could be," he said.

Beck became thoughtful for a moment. "You know, she knew the author from high school, and I heard her say she wanted to catch up with her afterward. Maybe she's with her. She's staying at the Manatee Beach Hotel."

"That's where we're staying," his wife said.

"That must be it. Maybe she's in her room," the man said, the relief palpable in his voice. "We tried calling her, but she must have her phone turned off because she didn't pick up."

"That could very well be," Beck said. "We asked everyone to silence their phones during the author's talk."

Beck saw relief and hope enter the man's eyes.

A thought occurred to Beck. "Wait, I have the author's cell phone number in my office. How about if I call her to see if your mother is with her?"

"Would you?" Joe Davidson asked eagerly. "I'm really starting to get worried. It's after ten o'clock. She's never out this late."

Beck returned to her office and made the phone call. Judging by the loud background noise, it sounded like Marcia Graybill was in the cocktail lounge of the hotel.

"Hello, Ms. Graybill," Beck said, talking louder than usual so the author could hear her. "It's Beck. Beck from the bookstore."

"Who?" The background noise was so loud, Beck could barely hear her.

"Beck. Beck from the bookstore," she repeated.

"Oh, Beck!" Ms. Graybill shouted into the phone as if Beck were her oldest, dearest friend in the world. "Dear, dear, Beck. How are you, Beck?"

Beck held the phone away from her ear. "I'm fine, Ms. Graybill," she answered. "I'm just calling because we're looking for the woman who said she went to high school with you. We can't find her and thought she might be with you."

"Her? I don't like her." The author's words were so slurred that Beck guessed she must be at least three or four martinis in. "She was mean to me in high school. They all were."

Yikes, Beck thought. Wonder what that was all about. "You haven't seen her then? We thought she might be with you."

"With me? Why would she be with me? I don't like her," she muttered incoherently. "I don't like her at all."

"Okay, then," Beck told the tipsy woman. "Thank you and have a nice evening."

"I'm having a wonnerful evening," she said thickly. "Just wonnerful. And the book signing was wonnerful."

"I'm so glad. Thank you, Ms. Graybill," Beck said, trying to break the connection.

"I'm having a really, really wonnerful time."

"That's nice, Ms. Graybill," Beck replied. "I really have to go now."

"Wonnerful."

"Bye-bye." Beck hung up and chuckled to herself. The author was absolutely blitzed.

When she returned to the couple at the door, Joe Davidson's hopeful gaze fell the moment he saw Beck's face. "I'm sorry, she hasn't seen her," she told them.

"Is there anywhere else she might be?" his wife asked Beck. "It looks like all the stores are closed."

"All of the nicer restaurants are closed by now," Beck said. "There might be a few bars open. Any chance she might have gone to one of those?"

"Oh, no," Joe answered quickly. "My mother doesn't drink."

Grammy appeared on the staircase, her fuzzy blue bathrobe wrapped snugly around her. "What's going on?" she asked.

Beck sent a worried glance toward Joe Davidson before telling her grandmother.

"It looks like Peggy Davidson is missing."

Chapter Eight

"Peggy Davidson?" Grammy asked.

"You remember, Grammy. Peggy was the woman who was so afraid of Coquina."

Her grandmother's eyes lit up in recognition. "Oh, yes. The woman with the beautiful emerald ring."

Lisa Davidson nodded. "Yes, that's her. When we got back to the hotel after dinner, we expected her to be back at the hotel. But she wasn't there."

"We've checked everywhere," her husband said. "She wasn't in the restaurant, the workout room, the pool. It's just not like her to be out this late."

Beck and her grandmother exchanged worried glances, and it was apparent they were both thinking the same thing. A string of murders the year before took place at the town's most vulnerable spot after dark.

"She wouldn't have gone out on the beach, would she?" Grammy asked them. "That's not a safe place to be alone at night."

The couple peered at each other. "I don't think so," Lisa said. "My mother-in-law is very cautious."

"No," the missing woman's son said, shaking his head. "She wouldn't have gone out onto the beach at night by herself."

Grammy suggested what Beck was thinking. "Maybe you should call the police."

"Oh, I don't think—" Lisa began.

Her husband seemed unsure. "Why don't we give it a little more time and keep looking," he said, as he turned toward the door. "Hopefully, she'll show up soon. Thank you for your help."

After they left, Beck locked the door and turned off the lights.

"Strange," Beck said. "I hope she's okay. I can't imagine where she could be."

Grammy didn't seem worried. "Oh, she'll turn up. She's probably off in some cozy corner reading one of Marcia Graybill's books."

She yawned and started toward the staircase. “Let’s get to bed. It’s late and we need to be up early. Another day, another dollar.”

Upstairs, Grammy told Lizzie they were going to bed, and it was time for Teddy to leave. Lizzie didn’t argue, as she sometimes did.

“I’m on early shift tomorrow, so I’d better get some sleep,” Lizzie told Teddy with a yawn, turning off the television.

“I’ll walk down with you, Teddy,” Beck said. “I need to take Coquina for her walk.”

Beck found Coquina’s leash, strapped it around her neck, and was practically dragged down the stairs by the dog who was anxious for her walk. Teddy hugged Lizzie goodbye and followed Beck downstairs.

At the door, Beck thanked him again for helping out. “I was happy to help,” he said with a grin, his dimples appearing. “Have a nice night.”

She watched him walk down the street to his vintage yellow Mustang convertible and take off. He and Lizzie must have such good time tooling around town in that car, Beck thought, with a tinge of envy.

Coquina took her time sniffing what seemed like every blade of grass before she finally did her business and didn't resist when Beck opened the front door and pulled her inside. She locked the door and turned off the lights for the third time that night.

Exhausted, Beck fell asleep quickly and was sleeping soundly when she was awakened by flashing lights and loud voices in the alley behind the store. She squinted at her alarm clock. Ten minutes after two a.m.

Lizzie appeared in her doorway wearing an oversized Miami Dolphins t-shirt and asked groggily, "What in the world is going on out there?"

Beck sat up in bed and narrowed her eyes at the flashing red lights that strobed across her window pane. Her room provided a better view of the back alley than Lizzie's. Together, they pushed up the wooden window frame and leaned out to look.

Four police cars, their headlights and flashers on, were parked at different angles aiming their high beams toward the back of the jewelry store next door. Beck's immediate thought was that the store had been robbed. Hurrying to her closet, she pulled on a pair of leggings and a long Florida State sweatshirt.

"I'm going down," she said.

“Wait for me!” Lizzie called after her. She ran back to her bedroom, quickly pulled on a pair of gym shorts, and caught up with Beck at the front door.

“Is Grammy awake?” Beck asked.

Lizzie shook her head. “When she has her fan on, she can sleep through anything. Coquina’s in there with her. She’s asleep, too.”

There was a chill in the air and a steady breeze off the ocean when they stepped outside. Beck hugged her body and was glad she’d put on a sweatshirt. As the sisters walked down the side alley between the stores, they saw an emergency vehicle pulled up behind the building.

“Somebody must be hurt,” Lizzie said.

When they reached the back of the building, aglow with light from the beams of the police cars, they saw the body. It was covered with a white sheet, but a woman’s foot wearing a dark blue pump stuck out from the end.

“Oh no,” Beck cried, immediately thinking of the missing woman from the book signing.

Lizzie, being a lifeguard, knew most of the EMTs, and approached a stocky paramedic who was leaning on the front of the emergency van.

“What’s going on, Gene? Who’s under that sheet?”

He nodded at her and straightened up. “Hey, Lizzie. It’s an older lady who was reported missing a couple of hours ago from the Manatee Beach Hotel. A tourist.”

Beck sucked in her breath. “Oh, my God, it’s Peggy Davidson!”

The paramedic turned to her in surprise. “Yeah, that’s the name. How did you know? Do you know her?”

“She came to our book signing tonight. Her son and daughter-in-law came over later and said they couldn’t find her. They were very worried about her.”

“You better tell the cops. The detective’s over there.” He pointed to a well-built, dark-haired man in a light-colored jacket. “Come with me.”

Beck realized immediately who the detective was, and wished there was some way, any way, she could avoid talking to him. But it didn’t appear there would be, and this poor woman’s murder was far more important than an embarrassing incident in college.

“Detective?” Gene said. “This woman has some information that may be helpful.”

When Devon Mathis turned around, he had the same effect on Beck he’d had over a decade ago when she was a freshman at Florida State University. He was as handsome a man as she’d ever laid eyes on—muscular build, square jaw, and thick lashes surrounding deep brown eyes. He always looked at her as if he were waiting for her to say something clever. So, naturally, feeling that she had to impress him, she became tongue-tied and nervous every time she was around him.

He'd been in the first criminology class she'd taken her freshman year. Growing up, she'd read so many mysteries and been so good at solving them that she thought she'd like to become a detective someday. But she felt like a little duckling out of water in those testosterone-heavy criminology classes back then. Totally intimidated. She, Devon, and another boy, a sophomore like Devon, worked on a team presentation together, on the fleeing felon law in Florida. She'd never forget it because she totally botched it. Froze in front of the class. Forgot everything—everything—and ruined it for all three of them. Some of the guys in the class even snickered at her. She heard one of them say, "Just what you need in an emergency situation." The whole group had gotten C's on the assignment because of her, and Devon seemed to avoid her after that. The rest of the semester, she felt embarrassed every time she went to class and couldn't wait until the term was over. To this day, before she spoke to a crowd of people, she thought about that awful day in criminology class.

Noticing her Florida State sweatshirt, Devon's eyes rose to her face and sparkled for a second in recognition. Then his lips curled into a half-smile. Was he still mocking her after all this time?

"Well, if it isn't my old team partner from FSU. Becky right?" he asked in the deep voice she remembered so well. "What brings you out in the middle of the night to a crime scene?"

Beck flushed, a wave of deep embarrassment flooding over her. He did remember her.

"Hi Devon," she said, avoiding his eyes. "I read in the newspaper that you were a detective here now. It's Beck, by the way."

"Beck. Okay. What are you up to these days, Beck? Obviously not law enforcement."

She felt her face grow hotter. She'd started to sweat. Was he making fun of her?

"No, I changed my major after—," she hesitated, "my freshman year. To literature." She looked up at him, finally making eye contact. "I own the bookstore next door, Beach Reads."

He glanced at the building. “Ah.” He sounded impressed. “I’ve passed by it many times. Looks like a nice place.”

“Thank you. That’s what I wanted to tell you.” She peered at the body and then quickly averted her eyes. “The woman there, Peggy Davidson, attended a book signing tonight at our bookstore. It may have been the last time anyone saw her. Her son and daughter-in-law came looking for her later. They couldn’t find her.”

“Hold on. Hold on,” he told her, pulling a narrow notepad from his inside coat pocket. He flipped it open and scribbled on it for several moments.

“Ok, so you say she was at a book signing tonight? Was she by herself or with someone?” He spoke without looking up.

“She was by herself. Her son and daughter-in-law weren’t interested so they went out to dinner while she was at the book signing.”

“No husband?” he asked.

“No, she was a widow.”

Devon continued taking notes. Beck found herself watching his hands as he wrote. They were so smooth, so strong. She wondered—

"Beck?" He was staring at her. "I asked what time this was tonight?"

She snapped out of her reverie. What in the world was she doing? A woman had died. A woman who had spent her last moments on earth in her bookstore. And here she was having romantic daydreams.

"Oh, uh, well, she arrived about seven o'clock or a little before and left around, eight-fifteen or maybe eight-thirty. I'm not sure. I was busy with the author so I wasn't really paying attention to her."

He glanced up from his notebook, his deep brown eyes penetrating hers. "Okay. So, let me get this straight. She left your bookstore between eight-fifteen and eight-thirty p.m. by herself and that was the last you saw her?"

The way he was looking at her made her nervous. Why did he still have that effect on her, even after all these years? She started to fumble her words.

"Well, I mean, I didn't see her leave, so I, I, mean, I don't know if she left by herself or if she, you know, was with someone."

She felt Lizzie's eyes on her. Her sister seemed to be enjoying watching her get flustered as she was being interviewed by this handsome cop.

The detective lifted an eyebrow and gave her a strange look. Then he continued, “And you say her son came to your bookstore to check on her later? What time was that?”

Beck struggled to get her composure back. She cleared her throat.

“I’d say they came by about ten o’clock looking for her. I had just finished doing some bookwork and was turning out the lights. She was supposed to meet them back at the hotel after the book signing, but she never showed up. They said they’d looked everywhere for her.”

She hesitated as he wrote down the information. Then she asked, “Have you contacted them yet?”

He shook his head. “No, not yet. They called in a missing person’s report about eleven-thirty, and we’ve had our people out looking for her. One of the officers found her about a half-hour ago. Looks like she’d been dragged around back from the side of the building.”

“What happened to her?” Lizzie asked.

Devon looked questioningly at Lizzie.

“This is my sister, Lizzie,” Beck told him.

He nodded at Lizzie. “She seems to have been hit over the head, at least once, maybe multiple times. With what, we don't know. We'll know more after the coroner's report."

Beck grimaced. "Was it a robbery? She was wearing a very expensive ring. An emerald."

Devon lifted his eyebrows in surprise.

"Oh really? Well, there's no ring there now."

"That's scary," Lizzie said, with a shiver. "Right next door to our house."

"Your house? I thought it was your store?" Devon said.

"Well, we live above the bookstore with our grandmother," Lizzie said.

"Hmm," Devon said, eyeing Beck. "A real family affair, huh?"

Beck winced. He must think she's the biggest loser in the world, still living at home with her family at twenty-nine years old.

Chapter Nine

The detective told her he would come by the bookstore the next day to get a more detailed report and said it would be best if she and Lizzie went back home while the police did their investigation.

"It's so awful," Beck said to Lizzie, as they climbed the stairs to the apartment.

"I know. It really creeps me out."

Lizzie followed Beck into her room and flopped on her bed while her sister changed back into her nightgown.

"I sure hope they catch whoever did it soon," Lizzie said.

Beck pulled off the sweatshirt and slipped her nightgown on over her head.

“Devon seems to know what he’s doing, so hopefully it won’t be long. The last thing we need is a mugger roaming the streets.”

Lizzie stretched out on her stomach and propped up her chin with her fists.

“So how do you know that detective anyway?” she asked, adding in a teasing tone, “*Devon.*”

Beck rolled her eyes. “We were in a class together many years ago during my freshman year at Florida State. It was a criminology class. When I first went to college, I wanted to major in criminology and become a detective.”

Lizzie’s curiosity was piqued. “That would have been so cool! Why didn’t you stick with it?”

Beck debated whether she should tell her sister or not. Becoming a police detective had been her dream throughout high school. She couldn’t wait to get to college to start taking the coursework she’d need to start a career in law enforcement.

“I just didn’t feel like I fit in. There were all these macho types in my class, you know jocks and frat boys, barely any other girls. It made me feel really uncomfortable.” Just remembering it was painful.

Lizzie frowned and curled her lips. “Why? Sounds like it would have been a lot of fun to me. I wouldn’t have felt uncomfortable at all. I woulda kicked their butts.”

Beck couldn’t help but laugh. “I’m sure you would have,” she agreed. “Sometimes I wish I had more of your personality.”

Lizzie smiled. She seemed to like that.

“But I was really shy back then,” Beck continued. “Painfully shy.”

Dropping out of the program had been crushing to Beck. Changing her major to literature felt like such a cop out, but law enforcement just seemed like too much of an uphill battle to her back then. Today, it would have been a different story. She had so much more confidence in herself now. But not when she was Lizzie’s age.

“You’re still kind of shy,” Lizzie said. “I could tell you were nervous talking to that cop. You like him, don’t you?”

Beck shook her head. “I don’t like him. He’s just an old classmate from college.”

“Yes, you do, and I can see why. He’s pretty hot. Maybe he’ll ask you out.”

Beck pursed her lips and shook her head again. “Trust me, he’s not going to ask me out.”

"You don't know that. You need to go out sometimes. When was the last time you had a date?"

"I don't know," Beck answered, irritably. "Anyway, that's your department, not mine."

Lizzie didn't let up.

"I can't even remember the last time you went out with somebody. The last person I can remember was that Darren guy, when I was like a sophomore in high school. What happened with him?"

"I don't know. What does it matter?"

Why couldn't Lizzie leave it alone? She didn't need this conversation in the middle of the night.

"C'mon what happened? He was always here and then poof, one day he was gone. I remember you got really cranky after that. You weren't easy to be around."

Beck tossed her sweatshirt into a chair and put her hands on her hips. "He dumped me, okay? Is that what you want to hear? He wanted to get married and I didn't, so he left and found somebody who did."

"You were too young to get married then."

"I know! Thank you."

"But just because some needy jerk dumped you, doesn't mean you have to give up on men forever."

“I haven’t given up forever. I’ve just been busy with the bookstore.”

Beck sat down on the edge of the bed. “Move over,” she said grumpily, giving her sister’s leg a shove.

Coquina ambled into the room, sleepy-eyed, and jumped up on the bed, taking what little space was left. The dog put her head in Beck’s lap. Beck rubbed her tummy, hoping her sister would drop the subject.

But Lizzie continued. “You haven’t been out with anybody since then, though. That was, like, three years ago!”

Beck groaned. “Like I said, Lizzie, I’ve been busy. And I haven’t met anybody interesting.”

Reaching out to scratch the dog’s head, Lizzie’s eyes brightened. “I can tell you like that detective guy. And I didn’t see a wedding ring. I looked. Maybe he’ll ask you out.”

Beck repeated more emphatically, “He’s not going to ask me out. I’m sure somebody who looks like him is beating women off with a stick. He probably has a girlfriend.”

“Maybe, and maybe not. Maybe he’s boring like you and only cares about his job.”

Beck peered up toward the ceiling. “Thank you, Lizzie.”

“All I’m saying is, you never know. He might be interested.”

“He’s not interested!” Beck almost shouted. “I blew that a long time ago.”

Now Lizzie was really interested. “What happened?”

“Never mind!”

“C’mon, Beck. What are sisters for? You can tell me anything. What happened?”

Beck debated whether she should tell her sister about the embarrassing incident during college. She sensed she would regret it if she did.

“C’mon,” Lizzie urged, reaching out to tickle her sister’s foot.

“Stop!” Beck giggled, pulling her foot away.

“C’mon.”

Beck sighed. “Well, if you must know, during my freshman year of college, Devon and I and this other guy had to make a presentation together in our criminology class. We worked really hard on it. I mean hours.”

She stopped and frowned up at the ceiling visualizing the classroom that day.

"I stayed up late preparing and didn't get much sleep. Besides that, I was so nervous. Just, so incredibly nervous. My first presentation in college."

"Ok, I get it. You were nervous," Lizzie said, leaning forward eagerly. "What happened?"

Beck cringed at the memory. She didn't even like thinking about it.

"Most of the class was guys, a lot of them sophomore and juniors, and I felt out of place anyway. Well, I was supposed to open the presentation, and I was so nervous I totally froze. I mean completely forgot everything I was supposed to say. A couple of the guys in the class started laughing at me, and that made it worse. I just stood there sweating, my face turned beet red, and I never said a word. Not one word. Devon and the other guy couldn't get us back on track, and we all ended up getting C's. Because of me."

"What a dork."

Beck picked up a pillow and flung it at Lizzie. She batted it away.

"Thanks a lot, Lizzie. I share the most embarrassing moment of my life with you and you make fun of me."

Lizzie let out a long sigh. "Okay. I'm sorry. But Jeez. Why didn't you just laugh it off, or make a joke out of it? That's what I would have done."

"Well, you and I are very different people. Anyway, in college, you can't just make a joke out of everything."

Lizzie thought for a moment. "So, this guy Devon was mad at you about it?"

"Well, he wasn't happy about it, but he didn't get mad at me or anything. But after that, he didn't talk to me too much. I just felt like such an idiot."

Lizzie stared at her for a few moments, thinking. "Well, I think you're making too much out of it. He probably doesn't even remember. That was ages ago."

"Oh, he remembers. I could tell by a couple of things he said tonight."

"That's stupid," Lizzie said, getting up off the bed and walking to the bedroom door. "If you like him, go for it."

Beck threw her pillow across the room at her sister. "I told you I don't like him."

Lizzie laughed. "For somebody who doesn't like him, you're getting awfully upset about it!"

She picked up the pillow and threw it back at Beck. It missed its target and landed on Coquina's leg. The dog bolted up, jumped off the bed, and ran out of the room.

Lizzie stepped through the doorway, and then leaned back in.

"If you need any advice about men, just ask me. I'm always available." Then she flitted off to her room.

Chapter Ten

Grammy was stunned by the news about Peggy Davidson.

"That poor, poor woman," she said early the next morning when Beck told her. Beck had barely slept a wink the entire night and got up at six a.m. when she heard her grandmother up and about.

"We need to go visit her son and daughter-in-law and give them our condolences," Grammy said, as she poured two mugs of coffee. "I'll pick up some extra muffins and scones, and we'll take them a basket."

She sat down at the small table in the apartment kitchen and set Beck's mug in front of the seat next to hers.

"Isn't it a bit soon, Grammy?" Beck began, sitting down and stirring her coffee.

Her grandmother stood up to get them both napkins, setting them on the bright yellow table cloth with the centerpiece of sunflowers.

"Not at all. In my day, you visited the bereaved right away so they'd know they had somebody to lean on. That poor man just lost his mother, and he's not at home where his friends and family can comfort him. We need to let him know we're here for them."

Leave it to Grammy to know the right thing to do, Beck thought. She might have a tough exterior, but she had the biggest heart of anyone Beck had ever known. Beck wanted to do something for the dead woman's son and daughter-in-law, too. She couldn't help feeling guilty and somewhat responsible. Mrs. Davidson had spent her last hours on earth at Beach Reads, and Beck had encouraged her to come to the book signing.

Beck and her grandmother decided against opening the bookstore that morning and waited until ten o'clock to go to the hotel to see the Davidson couple. When Grammy rapped on the couple's hotel room door, a haggard-looking, red-eyed Joe Davidson opened it. He seemed surprised to see them, but his wife walked up beside him and invited them into their suite, one of the nicest ones in the hotel. Grammy extended the basket of baked goods to Lisa Davidson, who seemed touched by the gesture.

"How nice of you," Lisa said, inviting them to sit down in a small living room area overlooking the ocean that contained a couch and two chairs. "Thank you for coming."

"We're just so sorry about your mother," Grammy told Joe. "Please accept our deepest condolences."

Appearing devastated, Joe nodded his head and stared at the floor. "I can't believe it. How could this happen?"

Lisa wrapped an arm around her weary husband's shoulder. "Joe didn't get a wink of sleep last night, he was so worried. Then, the police called about three in the morning to tell us they had news and would be right over. We're both still in shock."

Joe pulled his eyes away from the carpet and peered at Beck. "We just came down here for a little vacation. A break to look at some real estate. And now this?"

His eyes misted, and he swiped at them with the back of his hand.

Beck felt horrible for the poor man. And she couldn't stop thinking about their part in the tragedy. If only his mother had decided against coming to the book signing, she might still be alive.

"What did the police say?" Beck asked, directing her question to his wife. But Joe answered.

"Just that she was hit over the head with something and robbed. That her body was dragged behind the building." He choked out the last words. "I blame myself."

Lisa reached over to hug her husband. "He keeps saying that, even though none of this is his fault."

"We should have gone with her," Joe told them, almost as if he were asking them for forgiveness. "Or, at the very least, gone over there and walked her home. I should have taken better care of my mother."

Grammy patted his arm. "Now, now. Don't beat yourself up," she said sympathetically. "It's only a block between our bookstore and the hotel, and I walk out there a lot of times after dark. It's usually very safe. Nothing like this has ever happened before."

Lisa gave her a grateful look.

"If it's anyone's fault, it's mine," Lisa said to her husband. "Remember, after dinner, I stopped to shop in the souvenir shop right across the street from the bookstore while you went back to the hotel. I didn't even think to go over and see if she was ready to go back."

"It's nobody's fault," Grammy told them, "except for the criminal who robbed your mother. We're still in shock that it happened right next to our bookstore."

Joe stood up and strode to the window. Silently, with his hands in his pockets, he stared out at the breaking waves.

"The police won't even let us have her body to take home for 1burial," he said, after a few moments of silence. "They said they need to keep her for up to a week."

Lisa added, "And they told us we needed to stay here, too, while the investigation is going on, until they know more about what happened."

Grammy stood up and picked up her purse. Beck assumed it was time for them to leave, so she stood up, too.

"We want you both to know you have friends in town and that we're here for you if you need us," Grammy told them. "We feel terrible, just horrible, about what happened to your mother after she attended our book signing. You can call on us for anything you need. Anything."

She went to Lisa and hugged her and then did the same to her husband.

"Thank you," Lisa said. "That means a lot to us."

Beck gave them both a consoling hug, too, and then they left. As the two of them walked back to the store, Beck told her grandmother how impressed she was by the way she had handled the situation.

"When you get to be my age," the elderly woman said, "you've had a lot of experience dealing with the bereaved. When your grandfather died, having supportive people around helped me so much. I've never forgotten that, and I always try to be of help to others when I can."

As they approached the bookstore, Beck noticed the jewelry store next door hadn't opened yet either. But she caught a glimpse of the Merritts working inside through the window.

"Why don't we stop in to talk to them for a minute?"

"Do we have to?" Grammy groaned. "She'll probably just start complaining about something."

"Now, Grammy. I think it would be the neighborly thing to do," Beck said. "Afterall, it's not every day somebody gets murdered right outside your back door. I'm sure they're as upset as we are."

Her grandmother frowned, but then shrugged her shoulders. “As Lizzie would say, ‘Whatever,’” Grammy grumbled, conceding to her granddaughter’s wishes.

Beck tapped on the glass. Phil glanced up and immediately came to open the door.

“I guess you’ve heard the news,” he said. “The police were here earlier. Unbelievable.”

Lydia hurried over from behind the jewelry counter. “I was sitting right next to her at the book signing, and we walked right past our store when we left. It could have been me!”

Leave it to Lydia to make it all about her, Beck thought. Glancing at her grandmother, she could see she was thinking the same thing.

“What did the police say?” Beck asked.

“Not a lot,” Phil replied. “You know how the police are. They ask more than they tell. But we got the idea they thought it was a mugging.”

“Yes,” Lydia added, “they did mention she was wearing an expensive emerald ring that was stolen. That’s when I realized who it was. She showed it to us at the book signing. Very valuable.”

“I told them about the ring,” Beck said.

Lydia frowned and peered at her in surprise, as if Beck were stealing her thunder.

"You did?"

Beck nodded. "The police cars woke us up, so Lizzie and I went down in the middle of the night. About two o'clock."

Grammy piped up. "I missed all the excitement. Slept right through it."

"The police called us early this morning and asked us to come in," Phil told them. "You can imagine our shock. I wonder how long they're going to keep all that police tape up? They told us not to go out there."

"A few days, I'm sure," Beck said. "Until they've had time to thoroughly investigate the crime scene."

"Well, I hope they take it down soon," Lydia complained. "We can't get out the back door."

"Are you going to open today?" Grammy asked.

Lydia eyed her as if she couldn't understand why she'd ask such a stupid question.

"Of course, we're opening. In fact, Phil, go ahead and put the 'Open' sign in the window now. Who knows? Maybe it'll even help business."

After they left the store, Beck and her grandmother traded looks of disgust.

“Not a lot of sympathy for the poor dead woman she sat next to for an hour last night,” Beck said. “They were talking and seemed friendly.”

“I’ve known Lydia Merritt for a long time, Beck,” her grandmother told her, “and all she’s interested in is number one, herself, and number two, the almighty dollar.”

Chapter Eleven

Beach Reads had a larger than usual lunch crowd, and the main topic of conversation was the murder. Most people seemed convinced it was a mugging, and many of the women were adamant that they would not go out after dark until the culprit was caught.

As often was the case in Florida, the subject turned to guns. Beck wasn't surprised to hear that a few of their diners planned to head to the gun store immediately after they ate. One older patron, dressed in gym shorts and a tank top, lifted his shirt to display a revolver strapped around his waist.

"I'm carryin'," he said. "Let that mugger get near me, and he'll never know what hit him."

Beck hated guns and wouldn't have one in the store, though she had gone through an arms training course years earlier when she thought she was going into law enforcement. She wanted to find out if she could handle it. The feeling of having a weapon in her hand that could kill someone with just a tiny movement of her finger made her nervous and uncomfortable. But she was surprised to discover that she was a pretty good shot.

Beck was working the cash register, checking out the last of their lunch customers, when the front door opened and Detective Devon Mathis strolled in. He glanced around as if he were appraising the place, and then waved at her when he caught her eye. She held up her forefinger to let him know she'd be with him in a minute as soon as she finished with her customers. He held up his hand and pointed to the bookshelves, letting her know there was no hurry, that he'd be browsing the books.

After the last lunch customer left, Beck asked Grammy to mind the store while she talked to the police detective.

"I wouldn't be surprised if he wants to talk to you, too, Grammy," Beck told her, pointing him out across the room.

"Don't know if I'll be any help, but I'll be happy to talk to him." She elbowed Beck. "He's pretty easy on the eyes."

Beck laughed. Guess you were never too old to appreciate a fine male physique.

As she stood at the end of the bookshelf, studying Devon's profile as he intently flipped through the pages of a book, Beck couldn't have agreed with her grandmother more. With his tanned complexion, tawny brown hair that was just a tad too long, stubble of whiskers along that strong jawline, and his open jacket hanging casually from his lean frame, Devon Mathis was definitely easy on the eyes.

When he became aware of her watching him, he held up the book, Michael Connelly's latest.

"Bosch is the man," he said.

Beck grinned. "Michael Connelly is one of my favorites, too. That's a good one."

"Haven't read it yet. Think I'll buy it."

"You'll enjoy it," Beck said, walking over to stand beside him. "Classic Bosch. I think my favorite of his was *Angel Flight*."

Devon raised his eyebrows.

"*Angel Flight*. Oh yeah. Loved that one. My favorite though has to be *The Concrete Blonde*."

Beck nodded and gave him a knowing smile. "I liked that one, too."

She led him over to one of two armchairs in an alcove behind the bookshelves and motioned for him to take a seat. “Is this okay?” she asked, sitting down and crossing her legs.

“Fine, just fine. Nice place you have here. Very nice.”

“Well, thank you. I appreciate that.”

He sat down, setting the Michael Connelly paperback on the small end table between them.

Glancing down at the book, she said, “You know, Michael Connelly is from Florida. He was a newspaper reporter down in Ft. Lauderdale.”

“As a matter of fact, I did know that” Devon responded. “He got his journalism degree at that other big bad school.”

Beck laughed. He was referring to University of Florida, arch-rival of their alma mater Florida State.

“Oh well,” she joked. “You can’t have everything.”

Their conversation felt so natural. Until she thought about it, she wouldn’t have believed she wasn’t feeling nervous or tongue-tied at all around him. Maybe it was because she was on her own turf, in her bookstore, talking about books.

Coquina appeared and stood in front of them panting.

"Devon, meet Coquina."

His eyes widened a bit, but then he reached out and scratched the Great Dane between her ears.

"Coquina, huh," he said with a grin. "Pretty ironic."

"Oh, God," she thought. "He knows about irony, too."

"Can't think of a better name for a beach dog," he said, as he petted the big dog again.

Then he took out his notepad, searched his jacket for a pen, and pulled one out.

"Okay," he said, with a sigh. "Guess it's time to get down to business."

Beck folded her hands in her lap and leaned back in the chair. Coquina lay down on the carpet next to her. "Whatever I can do to help."

"What I'd like," he said, looking directly into her eyes, "is for you to tell me, step by step, from the beginning of the evening, about your book signing last night. Who was there, who interacted with the victim, what time people left the store. To the best of your recollection."

Beck let out a long breath. "That's a lot. Let me think."

Devon seemed to realize he needed to give her a prompt. "Let's start with how many people were there."

"I'd say at least fifty. It was one of our better-attended events."

"Who was the author?" he asked with interest. She could tell the question was more out of curiosity than of any pertinence to the case.

"Marcia Graybill. She's a cozy author."

He seemed disappointed. "Oh yeah. I've heard of her. But not my cup of tea, I guess you'd say."

Beck chuckled. "I understand. I don't think Harry Bosch fans are going to be into Marcia Graybill."

Devon shook his head. "No."

"But one interesting thing," Beck told him. "Peggy Davidson knew Marcia Graybill. They apparently went to high school together."

That caught the detective's attention. "Really? That is interesting."

"Yes, I thought so, too. Earlier that day, Peggy, her son, and her daughter-in-law came into the store to ask about the book signing. She told us then that she had gone to high school in North Carolina with a girl named

Marcia who she was pretty sure was Marcia Graybill. That was part of the reason Peggy wanted to come to the book signing."

The detective took notes and wanted to know more. "As far as you know, did the victim bring up to the author her belief that they attended high school together?"

Beck nodded. "Oh, yes. During Ms. Graybill's presentation, when she started talking about her difficult life when she was growing up in North Carolina, Peggy Davidson interrupted her to say they had gone to high school together."

"And how did the author react?"

Beck thought for a moment.

"You know, it was odd. It seemed to make her uncomfortable, and she barely responded to her. She just said something like, 'Isn't it a small world.' But nothing at all personal."

Devon took a moment to write some notes and then leaned forward, obviously interested in the connection between the two women.

"Did the two of them interact any more afterward that you noticed?" he asked.

"Oh, yes. Peggy got her book autographed by Ms. Graybill, and I took a picture of them together."

"What was their interaction like then?" the detective asked.

Beck gave it some careful thought so she'd tell him correctly. "I'd say, the same. Peggy was kind of gushing that she wanted to catch up, but the author looked uncomfortable, like she just wished Peggy would go away. Peggy said she would wait to talk to Ms. Graybill after she signed everyone else's books, but Ms. Graybill didn't respond. I could tell she didn't want to."

"And did they ever talk afterward?" he asked.

"No, not that I saw anyway," she said. "But when I talked to the author later by phone, when we were looking for Peggy Davidson and thought she might be with her, Ms. Graybill said she didn't like Peggy or any of the other girls she went to high school with. I don't know how much credibility you should give that though. Ms. Graybill was in the cocktail lounge in the hotel at the time and was definitely three sheets to the wind."

"Really?" Devon said, with a chuckle. "I guess a lot of people don't have fond memories of high school."

Beck nodded in agreement. There were a lot of moments from her high school days she'd just as soon forget.

Devon continued to jot notes as she talked, and was very interested in any interactions Peggy Davidson had.

"I did notice after Peggy had her book signed and was waiting to talk to Ms. Graybill that she had a long conversation with the author's husband. A couple of times when I looked up, I saw them talking as they waited for the book signing to be over."

"A long conversation with her husband, you say? What was their demeanor?"

Beck shrugged. "I don't know. Just a normal conversation."

"And did you see the victim after that? After the conversation with the author's husband?"

Beck shook her head. "I was busy with customers, but later when I looked up, Peggy was gone. I assumed she'd gotten tired of waiting. The book signing was going on forever."

She stopped to stare at Devon. "Why all the questions about Marcia Graybill and her husband? I thought Peggy Davidson was killed by a mugger."

Devon hesitated. "We thought so, too, initially. But we're beginning to think someone may have specifically targeted the victim and tried to make it look like a mugging."

Chapter Twelve

Beck couldn't hide her surprise. "What makes you think that?"

"Well, I can't go into a lot of detail, but the victim's head was battered more than a usual mugging victim would have been in a grab and run. Based on her head wounds, it was apparent that someone wanted this woman dead. It looked personal."

Beck's hands flew to her mouth. "Oh, my God. The poor woman. But who would want Peggy Davidson dead?"

Devon shrugged. "That's what we're trying to find out."

"But she was robbed too, right?" Beck asked. "Couldn't it have been a mugger who just went too far?"

"Possibly," Devon said, though he didn't sound convinced. "But the thing is, the only item that was stolen was that emerald ring. Her purse was strapped across her body and lying underneath her. She had a couple of hundred dollars in her wallet that wasn't taken. She also had on an expensive watch and a gold necklace that weren't touched either."

"Maybe the killer got interrupted," Beck suggested. "Or, somebody was just after the ring. She wasn't shy about showing it off."

"Really?"

Beck nodded. "My grandmother and I noticed it on her finger earlier in the day, and she loved showing it to us. She was very proud of it because her deceased husband had given it to her on their thirty-fifth wedding anniversary. I sensed that she was a little lonely, and I think remembering him by wearing the ring made her feel closer to him."

Devon caught her eye, and the way he squinted at her made her feel that he was judging her.

"And then, right before the author's talk," she continued, "when I was standing next to the front row waiting for my grandmother to finish a sale, I watched her showing it off to the people sitting around her."

That caught his attention. “And who was that?” he asked, his pen poised. “Who was she showing it to?”

“Well, I mean, I don’t think it’s anyone who would have done her any harm. It was our neighbors, Phil and Lydia Merritt, who own the jewelry store next door. They were making quite a fuss about it.”

He narrowed his eyes at her incredulously. “You mean the people who own the store where the body was found?”

A surprised look entered Beck’s eyes. “Well, yes, but I’m sure they didn’t have anything to do with it. They’re not my favorite people, but I don’t think they’d kill somebody for a ring.”

“Why aren’t they your favorite people?”

Beck suddenly felt uncomfortable. She didn’t want to get her neighbors into trouble with the police.

“Well, they’re always complaining that our customers are taking their parking spaces, or that food wrappers from our bookstore are on the sidewalk in front of their store.” She pursed her lips and shook her head. “You know, petty things like that. We were actually surprised they came to the book signing at all because they usually don’t have much to say to us. But apparently Lydia reads that author.”

"Hmm." Devon furrowed his brow and wrote something down.

"But I just can't believe they'd have anything to do with this. Anyway, it wouldn't be too smart to leave the body right behind your own store if you killed somebody." She looked at him questioningly. "Would it?"

He tilted his head and looked at her. "It would if you didn't have time to get rid of the body right away and were going to come back later."

The detective hesitated, and then told her, "Everything about this seemed rushed. Somebody clobbered her over the head, quickly dragged her body behind the store, and then snatched the ring. Maybe to come back later and finish the job."

"That may be true," Beck said, "but I just can't picture Lydia and Phil doing something like that."

Devon sent her a piercing gaze. "You never know what people are capable of."

He kept staring at her intently as he spoke. "By the way, I'm probably saying a little bit more than I should about the case because I know you from our criminology class in college. Needless to say, this is all confidential."

Well, that felt good, Beck thought. He thinks of me as kind of a peer because of my criminology background, short-term though it was.

“Oh, yes. Of course.” She made a zipper move across her lips.

Devon cleared his throat and said, “Okay, let’s start from the beginning. I’m not sure that it will matter, but it will help me to visualize the evening. Where were they seated?”

Beck stood up and he followed her. She led him the few steps across the room to the café side of the store and showed him how the seats and tables were rearranged for the book signing. She showed him how the backs of the chairs were to the bookshelves and to the left of the audience was the kitchen and cash register.

“Here was where the dais was located,” Beck said, standing in the spot where the author had spoken the night before. “I came out and introduced the speaker and then she spoke for forty minutes or so.”

His eyebrows went up, and he shot her a surprised glance.

“You introduced her?” he asked, with a little grin. “How’d that go?”

Beck colored and felt her confidence do a landslide. “Just fine, thank you,” she answered with an assuredness she didn’t feel.

A twinkle entered his eye. “You know, that class I took with you was the only B I got in my college major.”

She blushed but giggled at the same time. “Sorry about that.”

“Don’t worry,” he said, still smiling. “I’m over it.”

“Well, I’m glad to hear that.” She gave him a sheepish smile.

He was still grinning at her.

“Not my finest hour,” she said.

“No, I’m sure it wasn’t.”

“I’m a much better public speaker now. Really.”

“I’m sure you are. You’d pretty much have to be,” he teased.

She felt like swatting him. “Anyway,” she continued, drawing out the word, “Over here is where we had the table set up for Marcia Graybill to sign her books afterward.”

Grammy had been watching them curiously from the kitchen and decided to walk over to join the conversation.

"Grammy, this is Detective Devon Mathis," Beck said, adding, "Actually, we know each other from college."

"Hello, detective," she said, extending her hand. "I'm Miss Alice, Beck's grandmother and co-owner of this establishment. If I can be of any help, please let me know."

"Nice to meet you, Miss Alice." He gave her a polite smile. "Actually, you can be of assistance. Beck is setting up a reenactment of the book signing last night. If you remember anything specific, please don't be shy about letting me know."

Grammy's face lit up. "Oh, believe me. I won't be shy. I'm happy to help! Feel like I'm on *Columbo*!"

"Sorry I forgot my trench coat," Devon said with a grin. "Would you like me to leave and then turn around and come back in again?"

They all laughed, and Beck could see that Grammy was already a Devon fan.

"Okay, Beck," the detective said. "The speaker stood there giving her talk next to the table where she signed her books. Where was the victim sitting?"

Beck pointed in front of her. "Right there. Front and center, first row. She had the best seat in the house."

"And the jewelry store owners? Where were they?"

Grammy raised her eyebrows and her eyes widened. She mouthed "jewelry store owners" to Beck, who tried not to laugh.

"They were to her left. Lydia was sitting next to her and Phil was in the next seat down," Beck said.

"And on the other side?"

"My grandmother's friend, Dorothy," Beck told him. "Peggy showed her the ring, too."

"What is Dorothy's last name?"

Grammy spoke up. "It's Johnson. Is Dorothy a suspect? She'll love that."

Devon chuckled. "No, I'm just trying to learn who was sitting nearby. Do you remember who was sitting behind her?"

"I do," Grammy answered immediately. "That idiot Scratchoff McLean. He interrupted the woman's speech with a ridiculous question, and I had to tell him to sit down and be quiet."

"Scratchoff McLean?" Devon said, frowning. "That name rings a bell."

"He won the lottery," Beck reminded him. "The scratch-off lottery for a million dollars. He bought the Palms motel with it and fixed it up for homeless people to live in. He's definitely an odd character, but it was such a nice thing he did opening that motel for the homeless."

Devon's eyes lit up. "Oh, now I remember. Right before I first came on board here, he was under arrest for those beach murders."

"Yes," Beck said, reminding him, "but he was totally exonerated, and the real killer was eventually found."

The detective frowned and became thoughtful.

"But there was something else," Devon recalled. "If I remember right, he stole an emerald ring off one of the murdered women, didn't he? I don't think they ended up prosecuting him for it because of all the jail time he served. But he did take the ring."

"I don't really remember," Beck responded uncomfortably, annoyed with her grandmother for bringing up Scratchoff's name the way she did. "Scratchoff is definitely a colorful character, but he's not a murderer."

"Do you remember when Scratchoff left?" Devon asked, ignoring her comment about the former homeless man's innocence.

"Oh, he was the last one to leave," Beck told him. "It was about nine o'clock. He was waiting to take any leftovers we had back to the people at the motel. I walked him out with some tins of food and watched him ride his bike down the street."

The detective frowned. "And was he here the entire time? Could he have slipped out the door during the book signing?"

Beck didn't like the direction his questions were going. "I don't know. I wasn't paying attention to him. But I really think you're going down the wrong road with Scratchoff."

Grammy agreed. "That man gets on my last nerve," she said, "but I don't think he'd hurt a soul."

"Anyway," Beck said, "if he had left, killed her, and then come back here, he would have had blood all over him, wouldn't he?"

"Not necessarily," Devon responded. "In fact, probably not."

That was a surprise to Beck. "Why not?"

"Well, the wounds to the back of her head didn't bleed as much as you might think, and the victim wore a wig. Most of the blood was trapped under her wig."

"Hmm," Beck thought. It hadn't occurred to her that Peggy Davidson was wearing a wig, as a lot of women her age do when they don't have time to have their hair done. Being on vacation, she probably wore her wig after a day a beach.

Still, Beck was sure Devon was headed in the wrong direction suspecting Scratchoff. But he was making several notes, and Beck sensed that Scratchoff was now on his suspect list.

Next, he asked her who else was seated nearby. Beck named a couple of regular customers and then told him the rest were tourists that she didn't know.

"What happened after her talk?" Devon asked. Beck walked over to the wall at the front of the store, next to the front door.

"People lined up over here, to the right, to wait to have their books signed. It was kind of a slow process because some people had several books, and I took a picture of most of them with the author."

Devon stood up and strode toward the front door. "So, the line came along here, basically blocking the view of the front door and who was coming or going?" Beck studied it for a moment. "Well, yeah, I guess that's right. I hadn't thought about it that way, but I guess anyone could have left by the front door and been hidden by all the people standing in line."

"And where was the victim Peggy Davidson standing with Marcia Graybill's husband?" Devon asked.

Beck pointed. "Over there by the cash register."

Devon made a note and then asked her, "You say they had a prolonged conversation?"

"Yes. I looked up two or three times and noticed them still talking. Probably for at least ten minutes. But then I got really busy and didn't look over there for quite a while. The next time I did, they were both gone. I knew she was waiting to talk to Ms. Graybill, so I glanced around but didn't see her. I figured she got tired of waiting and left."

"And the author's husband? Where was he?"

"I didn't notice him, but I wasn't looking," she said. She glanced up toward the ceiling, thinking. "Oh wait. Later on, I noticed him sitting in that chair over there. But that was sometime later."

"Anything else unusual or noteworthy you can think of that happened," Devon asked both of them.

"Not that I can think of," Grammy said.

Beck thought about it for a moment and then shook her head. "No, not really. I was so busy coordinating the book signing that I didn't notice much. Sorry."

"Oh, no. All of this has been very helpful. Thank you." He flipped his notebook shut. "If either of you should think of anything else pertinent to the case, just give me a call." He handed each of them one of his cards.

He started for the door and then turned quickly around. "Oops, almost forgot to pay for the book."

"Oh darn," Grammy said. "I thought you were doing your *Columbo* thing."

Devon flashed her a radiant smile, his white teeth looking even brighter against his deeply tanned skin. He pointed his forefinger at her, "You're quite the pistol, Miss Alice. I'm gonna keep my eye on you!"

Grammy loved it and practically skipped back to the kitchen.

Beck rang up the purchase and handed him his change. "Enjoy," she told him.

"Oh, I will."

Exchanging one last glance with Beck and offering a hint of a smile, he turned away. And then he was gone.

Chapter Thirteen

The next afternoon, Beck was feeling stressed, claustrophobic, and on edge like she'd never been before. She needed to get out of the store for a while, breathe some fresh air, and try to clear her head. She decided to take Coquina for a walk. So much weighed on her mind. No matter how much she tried to talk herself out of it, she couldn't stop feeling guilty. She had encouraged a woman to come to a book signing at her store, and now that woman was dead, killed on her way home from the event.

Beck could think of nothing else. Was Peggy mugged, or did someone intentionally target her? Having such a vicious crime happen right outside your store, your home, was so frightening. After the string of murders in town the year before, those horrible knifings on the beach, she couldn't help but wonder if this murder was just the first one. Would there be more?

Taking her time as she strolled down Ocean Avenue, she let Coquina stop and sniff as much as she pleased. The Great Dane always got surprised looks and double takes from tourists who hadn't seen her before, but the shopkeepers along the way who were used to seeing her, either gave them a friendly wave or didn't give the dog a second look.

The street had a park-like feel to it. It was lined with sidewalks, flower boxes overflowing with bougainvillea, and plenty of comfortable white benches where husbands could enjoy nature while their wives hit the numerous dress shops. Royal palms, meticulously spaced apart, towered overhead. One of the nicest aspects about this area of Manatee Beach was that no chain stores were allowed. Every establishment was a specialty shop or restaurant owned by a local resident. The Manatee Beach Hotel sat in the center of the downtown area, anchoring the commercial section. It's oceanside, outdoor patio was a favorite lunch spot for tourists and locals alike.

Passing by the hotel, Beck glanced up and wondered how the Davidsons were doing. It must be so painful for them to have to stay here, waiting for permission to take his mother's body back to North Carolina. A twinge of guilt passed through her again. How horrible to go on a nice, family vacation and then have your mother get murdered. What a nightmare for them.

She took her time walking the dog two more blocks down Ocean Avenue, passing florist shops, real estate offices, and a few outdoor cafes, before turning east toward the beach. A minute later, she had her shoes in her hand and her toes in the sand. Manatee Beach was one of the few beaches along the South Florida coastline that allowed dogs on the beach. Coquina adored the beach, but Beck didn't take her there too often unless it was early in the morning or dusk. The big dog always caused a commotion with the kids. They either were scared to death of her or treated her like she was a pony. Some even tried jumping on her for a ride. Coquina was skittish, and the roughhousing of the children upset her. Not that she ever would hurt them—Beck was more concerned they would hurt her.

Being a weekday afternoon before school let out, the beach wasn't crowded, so they roamed along the water's edge relatively unbothered. It was a warm, cloudless day, the only shade coming from the occasional flock of pelicans that glided lazily overhead. Small groups of seagulls and sandpipers that scampered along the shoreline quickly fled as the Great Dane approached. Coquina liked the feel and smell of the wet sand, but she wasn't crazy about the water. Each time a wave broke too close to her, she galloped into the softer sand, and then warily worked her way back to the water's edge, only to repeat the process all over again.

When Beck saw Lizzie waving at her from atop the lifeguard stand down the beach, she tugged on Coquina's leash and crossed the warm sand to Lizzie's station. Not surprisingly, Teddy was sitting on one of the wooden cross beams of the lifeguard stand, his surfboard leaning against the base. Both of their beach bikes were chained to one of the rails.

Lizzie jumped off the stand, her tanned, athletic legs landing like a gymnast in the soft sand. As she gave the Great Dane a hug, Teddy walked over and started petting the dog, too.

"Hey, Beck! Wzup?" Lizzie asked. "You're not usually out walking Coquina at this time of day."

Beck shrugged and Lizzie could see that something was wrong. "What? What is it?"

"I just had to get out for a while. I'm so stressed out." Beck felt tears starting to well in her eyes.

"The murder? I know. It's so scary. Come here." Lizzie held open her arms. "Time for a sister hug."

Beck soaked up the warmth. She melted into her younger sister's arms.

"Okay," Lizzie whispered as Beck continued to cling to her. "Time to let go."

Beck released her and took a step back. "Thanks, I needed that."

"Anytime," Lizzie said, as she jumped up on the crossbar of the lifeguard stand and climbed agilely back up to the top. She quickly scanned the waves in both directions to be sure nothing had changed.

"I know it's scary having a mugger out there, Beck," Lizzie assured her, "but they'll catch him."

"Yeah," Teddy said. "They'll catch him. Don't worry."

"What's almost scarier, though," Beck said, "is that the police think Peggy Davidson may have been specifically targeted. That it wasn't a mugger."

That seemed to surprise both of them.

"How do you know?" Lizzie asked.

"I was interviewed today by the police detective."

Lizzie gave her a sly look. "The handsome one?"

Beck rolled her eyes. "Yes."

"What else did he say?"

Beck hesitated, remembering her promise. "I can't tell you. Devon told me some things in confidence."

"Oooooooh! Devon confided in you!" Lizzie said. "Maybe he likes you."

Beck let out a long breath of annoyance. Lizzie made her feel like she was in middle school. "He doesn't like me, Lizzie! Would you get over that? He just told me a few things because we took criminology classes together in college. I guess he figures I'm trustworthy," she said. "Which I am."

"Criminology? Did you want to be a cop?" Teddy asked. "You don't seem like somebody who would be a cop."

Beck shrugged. "Well, I wanted to be a detective. I guess I read too many detective stories growing up. But you have to be a cop on the street first before you can be a detective. I don't know how I would have done at that."

"I'm the one in the family who should be a cop," Lizzie said. "I'd wrestle those bad guys to the ground." She flexed a toned bicep.

"You know, Lizzie, you probably would make a good cop now that I think of it," Beck said.

Teddy sauntered over to his bike and began unchaining it. “I gotta head out.” He called up to Lizzie. “Movie tonight?”

“Um, maybe. Let’s talk later,” Lizzie said. They watched as he walked his bike, surfboard under his arm, through the soft sand to the hardpacked sand closer to the water’s edge. Then he jumped on his bike and rode off in the opposite direction of their house, the sun glinting off his nearly white hair.

“He seems really nice,” Beck said to Lizzie. “Is this one a keeper?”

Lizzie shrugged. “Who knows? He is nice, but there’s so many fish in that great big sea.” She spread out her arms to the ocean before her.

Beck shook her head. “You are too much, Lizzie! God forbid you should stay with someone for more than a week.”

“Who knows?” Lizzie said, with a laugh. “Maybe Teddy will make it to two.”

“Where does he live?” Beck asked as they watched him ride his bike toward the south end of town. “With his parents?”

"No, his parents died when he was in high school. He's kind of an orphan. No brothers or sisters either. He has his own apartment."

"That's sad," Beck said. "You should be extra nice to him if he doesn't have family."

"I am nice to him," Lizzie replied defensively. "What do you think?"

She suddenly jumped up, blew her whistle, and motioned to a pale-skinned swimmer who had gone out too deep to swim into shallower water.

"I have to watch these tourists like a hawk," Lizzie told her. "Some of them think they're a lot better swimmers than they are."

Lying in the shade underneath the lifeguard stand, Coquina had begun to pant heavily.

"I'd better get Coquina some water. She looks thirsty," Beck said, pulling on the dog's leash.

"There's a doggie water fountain down there," Lizzie said, pointing in the direction of the hotel.

Beck gazed down the beach and started moving in that direction. "Okay, we're going to go ahead and head back."

"Beck."

“Hmm?” Beck asked, shading her face with her hand to look up at her sister.

“Try not to stress out. The police will figure this out. Everything will be okay.”

“Thanks, Lizzie. I’ll try. But it’s not going to be easy.”

Chapter Fourteen

Three days had gone by, and it was as if the murder had never happened. News reports provided little new information about the case. Everything seemed to be completely back to normal except for the police tape that still stretched across the alley behind the bookstore.

In the daytime, that is. After the sun went down, it was a completely different story. The streets were quiet and businesses on Ocean Avenue closed early. Beck didn't venture out, and even Lizzie was staying closer to home. The nights had become downright eerie, and Beck found herself tossing and turning half the night as thoughts looped through her brain of Peggy Davidson alive at the book signing and then dead under that sheet. And the guilt wouldn't go away. If only Peggy hadn't come to the book signing, she'd probably be alive today.

It was a quiet afternoon and Beck was on a stepladder, shelving copies of the latest Nora Roberts novel, when the front door opened, and she heard the familiar voice of Scratchoff McLean. The store was empty, and Grammy was upstairs taking a nap.

"Miss Alice? Miss Beck?"

Beck descended the stepladder and poked her head around the corner of the bookshelf. "I'm over here, Scratchoff. Can I help you with something?"

His blond hair was long and tangled and looked like it hadn't been combed in days. He wore a pair of faded cutoff jeans and a torn purple t-shirt that pictured a pelican holding a fish in its mouth.

He stepped forward and gave her a perplexed look. "I was just wonderin' if I did somethin' to offend y'all for you to sick the po-lice on me?"

Beck wasn't sure if she'd heard him right.

"Sick the police on you? We didn't do that. We wouldn't do that."

"Well, that new young detective feller, one that took old Detective Weston's place, came and picked me up and had me down at the station for near four hours. Said he heard I was sittin' right behind that lady that died and had that great big ring on her finger."

Beck felt a tinge of guilt. She remembered her grandmother bringing up Scratchoff's name to Devon Mathis, but they weren't implying he should be a suspect. They just mentioned he was one of the people at the book signing who was sitting near the victim. Unfortunately, Devon seemed to take the information differently.

Beck told him that. "He wanted to know everybody who had attended and what time they left. Not just you."

That seemed to mollify him a bit.

"I reckon he looked to me because it was a emerald ring that was stole. I know that other time, last year, I kinda took that emerald ring offa that dead lady, but I didn't mean no harm. She was already dead, and it wasn't any use to her anymore. But I sure didn't hit no lady over the head with a brick just to steal her ring."

"A brick? That's what Peggy Davidson was hit with?" Beck immediately thought of the stack of bricks on the side of the bookstore, the leftovers from the patio they'd built last year.

Scratchoff nodded. "She wasn't hit just once, neither, from the sounds of it. More like four or five times."

Beck grimaced and felt sick to her stomach. Poor Mrs. Davidson.

"Like I tole you the other night, I'm tryin' to be a upstanding citizen in this town now that I won all that money and own the motel and all. Even payin' some taxes. But it's kinda hard if every time somebody gets killed around here they go draggin' me in thinkin' I did it."

He crossed his arms and peered down at the floor. Beck felt sorry for the man. He'd been wrongly accused once before, and that had to have taken its toll. She'd known him for years and just couldn't believe he was capable of such violence.

"I don't think they necessarily think you did it, Scratchoff. They're probably pretty much questioning everybody."

Scratchoff shook his head back and forth a couple of times.

"No ma'am. No ma'am. It sure didn't sound that way to me, Miss Beck. I thought they was gonna lock me up sure as I'm standin' here."

Now Beck really felt bad that his name had come up so prominently in their conversation with Devon.

"But they don't have any proof against you, do they? Other than the fact that you were here that night."

"They don't always need proof. If you remember last time, they locked me up for a good two months, thinking I killed those women. I kept tellin' em I didn't do it, but they wouldn't listen."

He crossed his arms and stared out the window. "'Course that was before I got respectable by winning all that money. Before that I was livin' behind them sand dunes down the beach sleepin' on an old raft. Back then, they didn't believe nothin' I said."

Beck had read every newspaper account and watched every news report about the three women who had been murdered on the beach a year before. She was well aware that Scratchoff was the primary suspect for weeks.

"I do remember when you were under arrest for those beach murders," Beck said. "But they released you after they found out you had a solid alibi and eventually found out who the real murderer was."

Scratchoff seemed pleased that she remembered.

"That's right, Miss Beck. I was unjustly accused once, and I'm afraid it's gonna happen to me agin."

A wistful look came over Scratchoff's face that surprised Beck.

"'Course I remember havin' some real good eatin' whilst I was locked up in that jail. And a comfortable bed, too, come to think of it. Kinda hated to leave there after I got used to it. But now, I got me my own microwave and hot plate in my little motel room, and I can cook my own food. Afford my own groceries, too. Don't need to go scrappin' around, if you know what I mean."

Beck knew exactly what he meant. She had a clear memory of him when he was homeless, wandering the streets checking out garbage bins and asking tourists for their spare change so he could buy scratch-off lottery tickets. She'd been shocked when she heard he'd actually won, but very happy for him. And the way he spent the money really impressed her, buying the motel so he and his homeless friends would have a place to live. He'd proven himself to have a good heart.

"What else did the police say?" she asked.

"Well, they were trying to get me to say I left the book signin' while it was still goin' on because they seem pretty sure that lady was attacked right after she left here."

"I wonder how they know that?" Beck asked with a frown. She had hoped the woman might have gone back to her hotel and then gone out again, so her death wouldn't be so directly related to their book signing—so Beck wouldn't feel so much guilt.

Scratchoff was quick to answer. "They think that cause she was still carryin' the book that writer lady had signed for her."

"Oh," Beck murmured, letting the grim reality set in that Peggy Davidson had been killed seconds after she left their bookstore.

"But I tole them I never did leave the store." He pointed toward the snack bar. "I stood over there at the end of that counter waitin' for everthin' to finish up so I could get those brownies. You remember, don't you, Miss Beck?"

She wished she could give him an iron-clad alibi, but she couldn't.

"I saw you standing there when I glanced over, but honestly, Scratchoff, I was so busy with the book signing, that I couldn't say you were there the whole time."

He looked disappointed and scratched his head.

"But if you say you were, of course, I believe you," Beck added.

His face lit up at her comment, and he seemed sincerely touched.

"Maybe Miss Alice could tell them I was there? She was in the kitchen most of the time. 'Course she was tryin' to ignore me as best she could. All she said to me the whole time was why didn't I buy a book for the author to sign."

"And what did you tell her?" Beck asked him, more curious about what he said than anything else. He never bought anything. Old habits die hard.

"Well, I tole her that I'm not much of a reader, but I surely do like takin' part in town activities."

Beck chuckled. "And what did Grammy say to that?"

"She didn't look too happy with me. Kinda shook her head and didn't say nothin' else to me. But she knew I was there the whole time, and it sure would be helpful to me if she'd tell that to the detective feller."

Beck glanced toward the staircase. "She's upstairs taking a nap now, but I'll let her know you asked."

"I'd be mighty thankful if you'd do that. I don't need the po-lice on my back again. I had enough of that last year to last a lifetime."

He waved goodbye, and she watched him climb onto his bike and ride off down the street. After her conversation with him, though, she felt so much worse than she did before. Peggy Davidson walked out the door of their book signing and had the life beaten out of her with a brick. Beck couldn't get over the thought that if the poor woman hadn't come to their book signing, she'd probably still be alive today.

Chapter Fifteen

It must have been her afternoon to get rebuked for talking to the detective because not a half-hour after Scratchoff left the store, Lydia from next door arrived in full rage.

Thank goodness there were no customers in the store when she arrived. Grammy had just awoken from her nap and was in the bookstore kitchen making them both a cup of tea. Sitting at the counter chatting with her grandmother, Beck whirled around when she heard the front door slam.

Lydia marched across the store to the snack bar and, as was her way, didn't bother with pleasantries. She got right to the point. "Just what have you been saying to the police about Phil and me?"

Before Beck had a chance to respond, Grammy stepped forward, ready for battle with her least favorite neighbor.

"What in the world are you talking about, Lydia?"

Lydia put her hands on her hips and glared at Beck and her grandmother.

"You know exactly what I'm talking about, Alice O'Rourke. That police detective made us go down to the police station for an interrogation. The police station! Can you imagine?"

Beck could see the corners of her grandmother's mouth start to turn up, as well as the tension in her cheeks as she struggled not to smile. There was no doubt she was enjoying this. "Well, the body was found behind your store. What do you expect?"

Lydia glared at Grammy, her eyes bulging.

"That interview went way beyond the coincidence that her body was dragged behind our store," Lydia huffed. "That detective, whatever his name is, said he'd been told we were showing interest in her emerald ring at the book signing. He acted like we killed her to take it. Who else would have told him that but you? I saw him over here talking to you the other day."

Grammy shrugged. "If you don't have anything to hide, I don't know what you're so hot and bothered about."

Lydia looked like she might take a leap at Grammy's throat, so Beck jumped in to try to calm down the situation.

"Now, Lydia, Detective Mathis just asked us where Peggy Davidson was sitting, and who she interacted with. We couldn't hold back information in a murder investigation. We told him everything we observed. We mentioned several names, not just yours."

That did little to soothe Lydia's temper. She was still fit to be tied.

"Do you know that detective had the nerve to go into our bank accounts?"

Grammy eyes widened and she stifled a laugh, but Lydia heard it and turned on her.

"You think that's funny? How would you like it if the police started questioning you about how much money your business makes?"

Grammy wasn't about to give Lydia any support. She was a Devon fan all the way.

"I'm sure that nice detective has a perfectly good reason for everything he's doing. He seems very capable to me."

If Grammy were fifty years younger, Beck was sure she'd have a major crush on Devon Mathis. She might have one anyway. Nothing negative about him would leave her lips.

Lydia realized she wasn't going to get any sympathy from Grammy, so she turned to Beck for support.

"He practically accused us of murder. Can you believe that? He implied we killed her for that ring and then hid her body behind the store until we could come back later in the night to get rid of her. Can you imagine? I thought poor Phil was going to have a heart attack right there on the spot."

Beck didn't know what to say. She was stunned herself that Devon would so blatantly imply that Phil and Lydia had committed murder. Yes, the body was found behind their jewelry store, but still. What Lydia told them about the police checking their bank accounts did make her wonder, though. There had been speculation that their jewelry store wasn't doing well and might have to close. Did Devon think they might have stolen the ring to keep their store afloat? The ring had to be extremely valuable, so maybe that was his theory.

"I'm sure the police are just investigating every possible avenue," Beck said, thinking of her talk with Scratchoff. "I've heard they've interviewed other people, as well."

Lydia didn't seem to be listening. Beck had never seen her so wound up.

"Well, you know who they should be looking into if you ask me?" the jewelry store owner said.

"Who?" Beck asked, suddenly very interested in her reply.

"That daughter-in-law of hers. Lisa Davidson."

Grammy frowned in disbelief and challenged her. "Why would you say that? That poor woman and her husband are totally broken up about his mother's death. We went to visit them the morning after it happened, and if you had seen how upset they were, you wouldn't be saying that."

Lydia lifted her chin and looked at them with disdain.

"Well, she certainly seems to have gotten over it fast. Looks to me like she's already spending her husband's inheritance."

"What do you mean?" Beck asked.

"She came into our store this afternoon and bought a ten thousand dollar diamond bracelet. She wasn't shedding any tears about her poor departed mother-in-law then."

Beck and her grandmother exchanged surprised glances.

"That is a surprise," Beck said. "Was her husband with her?"

Lydia shook her head. "No, she said he was still too upset to leave the hotel. She was getting bored sitting around the room, so she decided to go shopping. They have to wait in town until the police release the body."

The front door opened and a woman wearing a batik cover-up, carrying a beach bag came in. When Beck started toward her, the woman waved her off saying she was just looking for a book for the beach. Beck left her to it.

When Beck returned to her grandmother and Lydia at the counter, she asked them to lower their voices.

"From the way she was talking," Lydia whispered loudly, picking up the conversation where she'd left off, "the estate they're inheriting is huge. Millions. Her husband is an only child so they get it all."

Beck frowned distastefully. "So, Lisa Davidson was bragging about the inheritance to you?"

Lydia hesitated and looked a little uncomfortable. She chose her words carefully.

"Well, I wouldn't say she was bragging. I was just curious, you know? So, I asked some subtle questions. I needed to know her income level so I could direct her to the right price range of merchandise."

Beck pursed her lips. How nosy could you get, grilling a bereaved woman about her inheritance a couple of days after her relative's murder?

But Grammy had a nosy side too, especially when she thought Lydia knew something she didn't.

"So, how much are they inheriting?" she asked bluntly.

Lydia seemed to be enjoying having information that Grammy didn't, and looked like she might not say. But the tidbit was far too titillating for her to keep to herself.

"Well," she said, lowering her voice as if it were a valuable secret, "apparently her father-in-law was CEO of a huge engineering company and was worth nearly one hundred million dollars. They own property all over the place, and their home in North Carolina is supposedly quite the mansion."

Grammy whistled at the sum. "I thought they must be pretty well off based on the size of that emerald ring."

"Oh," Lydia added with a note of glee in her voice, as if she'd forgotten the best part, "apparently he paid over two hundred thousand dollars for that ring. I knew it was one of a kind."

The look Beck gave her must have reminded Lydia that she was under suspicion of murder because of that ring. Lydia's face colored, the look of delight left her eyes, and she began fiddling self-consciously with a wisp of hair that had fallen from the tight bun she always wore. She quickly turned away from them and started toward the door.

"Did you tell the police all this?" Beck asked her.

She stopped and turned back.

"No. I didn't know then. She came in the store right after we got back from the police station," Lydia said. Lifting her chin, she added, "And as far as the police are concerned, I don't care if I ever talk to them again. They can find out for themselves."

Chapter Sixteen

After Lydia left, Beck and Grammy sat down at the counter for a cup of tea and a scone. Their only customer finally bought a book and left, so they wanted to take advantage of a few minutes to themselves before the after-beach crowd arrived.

Grammy still couldn't get over Lydia's tirade. "Can you believe Lydia grilling poor Lisa Davidson about how much money they were going to inherit when her mother-in-law isn't even warm in her grave?"

Beck shook her head, stirring her tea. "Just because Lisa does some shopping to pass the time while they're required to stay in town, doesn't mean she's callous about her mother-in-law's death. Buying a diamond bracelet like that to her is like you or me buying a new hat. You could tell she and her husband had a lot of money on their own without his mother's fortune."

A flicker of a smile crept across Grammy's face, and Beck couldn't help smiling, too. "What are you finding so amusing, Grammy, as if I didn't know?"

Grammy gazed at the ceiling. "I'm just trying to imagine old Lydia being taken into some bleak interrogation room, sitting in a hard chair behind a metal table, being grilled by the police. I sure would love to have been a fly on the wall for that."

Beck laughed. "I knew that's what you were thinking! You're terrible."

"That made my week!" Grammy said. "Good for Devon. I knew I liked that man."

As if on cue, the door opened and Detective Devon Mathis appeared. It had been quite the revolving door of suspects today, and now the detective, too.

Grammy immediately jumped to her feet to welcome Devon.

"Well, c'mon in. How about a cup of coffee?" she asked, as he took a seat at the counter.

"Don't mind if I do," he replied with a wink. Beck was sure her grandmother had actually blushed.

He turned to Beck and gave her a friendly nod, "Hello, Beck."

She smiled in return and felt her heartbeat speed up. His presence seemed to fill the entire room.

Grammy poured him a cup of coffee and told him, "Now I know you guys like donuts, but we don't have any of those. How about a Danish?"

Devon grinned and shook his forefinger at her. "Now, now, that donut thing is just a stereotype. I've always been a Danish man myself."

"I had you figured for that," Grammy said, choosing the largest apple Danish left under the glass dome for him.

Beck was surprised at how excited she felt to see him again. He was beginning to feel more like a friend than just a policeman doing his job. For a moment, she wondered if he'd stopped in for a social visit rather than for police business.

Sipping on his coffee, Devon seemed to be relishing the afternoon treat when Beck asked him, "How's the new Michael Connelly book? Have you had a chance to start reading it yet?"

He wiped his mouth with a napkin and shook his head. "I wish. This investigation is taking all of my time."

"Yes, it seems like you've had a busy week from the sounds of it."

He raised his eyebrows at her. "Sounds of what?"

When she told him about their afternoon visits from Scratchoff and Lydia, he didn't respond. So, she continued. "They both seemed to think that we put you on to them." Her tone held a small rebuke. "They weren't very happy with us."

He turned toward her and made eye contact. "Just doing my job. I didn't mention you, but I guess they figured that out on their own. Didn't mean to cause a problem for you."

Grammy was quick to side with Devon. "How's he going to find the killer if he doesn't pull in some of the likely suspects? I hope you made Lydia squirm." She leaned across the counter closer to him and whispered, "Do you think she did it?"

He chuckled. "We're not ready to make any arrests yet. Just trying to gather as much information as we can. Which is why I'm here."

So, this was an official call and not just a social one. Beck felt a little disappointed.

Grammy took his empty plate and refilled his coffee cup. "Shoot," she said. "We'll help you out in any way we can."

He took his notepad out of his jacket and set it down on the counter. "Miss Alice," he said, clicking his ballpoint pen, "after the book signing on the night of the murder, do you recall if Scratchoff McLean left this counter at any time before the end of the evening?"

Beck found herself irritated by the question and wished she'd had a chance to ask her grandmother that same question as she'd promised Scratchoff she would. Now, the question was coming directly from the police, catching Grammy off-guard.

"Well, now, let me think. I noticed him down at that end of the counter," she said, gesturing to the far end of the snack bar, "but there were a lot of people standing around that night, eating brownies, and drinking coffee. I didn't pay much attention to him. He never buys anything, so I usually pretty much ignore him."

"Could he possibly have left the bookstore and then come back?" the detective asked her.

Grammy shrugged. "I don't know. Maybe. The few times I glanced down there, I think he was there. But I couldn't swear to it."

Devon turned his attention to Beck. "How about you, Beck? Did you notice him here the entire time?"

Beck shook her head. "Like I told you before, I was so busy with the book signing, I didn't notice that much. I did see him at the counter a couple of times, but I couldn't swear he was there the entire time."

As Devon made some notes, Beck couldn't help adding, "But honestly, Devon, I really think you're going down the wrong path with Scratchoff. He's a real character and is definitely a little odd, but he's not dangerous."

She could tell Devon didn't like the comment, and he sent her what she considered a patronizing look—like she didn't know what she was talking about.

"We have our methods," was all he said in a dismissive tone.

His words and his attitude didn't sit right with her, and she stiffened. She had a flashback to that criminology class where those jocks and frat boys treated her like she was less than. He was a jock just like the rest of them—a baseball player. Her face flushed as she remembered how her dreams of becoming a detective had been shattered in that class. She'd been such a shy, awkward girl back then. And not tough enough. Definitely not tough enough. She knew, though, she just knew, that if she hadn't felt so put down back then that she could have become as good a detective as any of them. Better. She had a knack for it. She always had. She was always the first one to figure things out.

Her cheeks on fire, Beck stood up. "If that'll be all…"

He jerked his head and peered at her in surprise. "Well, no," he said. "I do have another question."

"What is it then?" she asked impatiently. She knew her anger was at the boiling point and, if she didn't get away from him quickly, all the rage she'd felt for years would spill out.

He frowned and gave her a perplexed look. Clearly, he didn't understand what had upset her.

He cleared his throat. "The other question I have concerns the author, Marcia Graybill, and her husband. We have contacted them about coming in for questioning, but she's refusing. They're in Miami now on her book tour, and they're scheduled to go on to Key West next."

The fact that Marcia Graybill was refusing to come back to Manatee Beach to be questioned by the police didn't surprise Beck at all. Marcia Graybill was going to do exactly what Marcia Graybill wanted to do when Marcia Graybill wanted to do it.

"What do you want to know?" Beck asked brusquely.

Still appearing taken aback by her tone, he asked her, "You told me the last time we talked that you noticed Peggy Davidson speaking at length with the author's husband."

Beck nodded without looking at him.

"Is that the last time you saw her?"

"I told you it was."

Devon flinched a little at her terse response. He lifted an eyebrow and gave her a bewildered look. He seemed confused about where this conversation had gone south.

"Could the author or her husband possibly have left the book signing about the same time the victim did?"

Beck frowned. "Well, Marcia Graybill certainly couldn't have. I watched her sign books for well over an hour for thirty people. She never left the table."

"And her husband?" Devon asked.

"I don't know about him. I noticed him talking to Peggy, and then I really didn't see him again until twenty or thirty minutes later. So, I just don't know. I suppose it's possible."

As Devon jotted down several notes, she looked away. When she glanced back, she noticed him studying her. He quickly closed his notebook and stood up.

"All right. Thank you for the information."

But Beck wanted to know more, and she had a question for him now. "So, I take it you think Peggy Davidson was hit over the head with a brick right after she left the bookstore, on her way back to the hotel? Because she still had her signed copy of the book with her?"

Devon gave her a stern look. Those deep brown eyes seemed to be boring into her soul. "How did you know that?"

"It's a small town. Word gets back."

He pursed his lips. She knew she'd blown any chance of him ever confiding information in her again. And she didn't care. This crime had happened right outside of her store after an event that she had hosted. The poor woman was even killed with a brick from their own brick pile. Beck needed to resolve the feelings of guilt that were haunting her. She had to know what happened. She had to be able to give the murdered woman's son some peace.

The police clearly were going in the wrong direction. About that, she felt confident. She made the decision right then and there that she was going to do some sleuthing herself. She knew she could solve crimes as well as any of those college boys who had taken her dream away from her. She wasn't that shy girl with no self-confidence anymore. She may not have been tough enough then, but she was tough enough now.

Devon turned to Grammy. "Thank you for the coffee and Danish, Miss Alice."

"You come back anytime, detective," Grammy replied gaily, apparently unaware of the coldness that had passed between Devon and Beck.

He gave Beck a sharp look and a nod. "Beck." And he was out the door.

Chapter Seventeen

As soon as he left, Beck ran up the stairs to her bedroom, feeling so emotional that she was sure she would burst into tears. Surely, she'd blown any chance she had with the first man she'd felt any attraction to in years. But, strangely, the opposite happened. A euphoria came over her, and she started laughing. She felt more exhilarated than she had in a long time.

Lying back on her bed, her fingers interlaced behind her head, she stared up at the ceiling fan whirring above her and tried to figure out why she felt so good. It took a while, but she finally realized what it was. Her passion was back. Owning the bookstore was a pleasant job that fulfilled her to a point, but it wasn't her passion. That dream of doing detective work that she'd felt so fervent about for years had never really left her. And now, it was going to become a reality. She would make it a reality. Of course, she wouldn't be doing it officially, but she was going to investigate this case that hit so close to home on her own. She definitely had the instincts, and she had the background, both from the thousands of crime novels she'd read, as well as from her brief studies of criminology in college.

Concentrating on the case at hand, Beck thought about the crime scene and how Peggy Davidson was killed. The victim left the book signing and someone either followed her or was lying in wait. Killing her seemed to be an instantaneous decision because the killer didn't have a weapon beforehand. Whoever it was, he or she grabbed the brick and followed her. Mrs. Davidson was older and overweight and wouldn't have been able to move quickly enough to escape someone who was chasing her. The shops near the jewelry store were closed, so there may not have been anyone on the street at that time to notice anything.

The killer probably came up behind her and forced her into the alley on the other side of the jewelry store. Then, the murderer knocked her out with the brick and continued to beat her with it to be sure she was dead. Beck mulled the situation over in her mind and decided the overkill would have taken place for one of two reasons. Either stealing the ring was the motive and the robber realized Mrs. Davidson recognized him or her, so she had to be killed. Or, doing away with Mrs. Davidson was the goal all along, and stealing the ring was an afterthought or a diversion.

Beck wasn't sure which was the case, but Devon and the police department seemed focused on the theft of the emerald ring, based on his interviews with both Scratchoff and Lydia and her husband. If one of them was the killer, what other reason could they have to want her dead other than she might be able to identify them? None of them had met her before that night, or in Scratchoff's case, just sat close to her.

On the other hand, if Mrs. Davidson was killed because someone specifically wanted her dead, that would imply the person knew her before the night of the book signing. The woman was a tourist, visiting Manatee Beach for the first time. Beck doubted anyone she'd met since she'd been on vacation would specifically target her for death unless, perhaps, she knew someone who lived in this area. The key, Beck decided, was to get to know more about Peggy Davidson's life, past and present. And that's what she intended to do. She had a starting place now, and she felt more excited, exhilarated, than she had in a long time.

Beck stayed upstairs longer than she intended, and when she went back downstairs, she found Grammy waiting on two tables of customers who obviously had just spent the day at the beach. One party was a mother with two squirming preschool-age children, who had filled the fourth empty chair at their table with sand buckets and shovels, towels, and a carry bag stuffed with flippers, arm floaties, and other beach gear. At another table were four giggling teenage girls, all wearing something that qualified as a cover-up, though a couple of them were pretty scanty. Grammy had a firm rule about no bathing suits in the store and that men must wear a shirt. A sign to that effect was posted on the front door.

"Where have you been?" Grammy asked as she poured four tall glasses of lemonade for the teenage girls. "Are you feeling okay?"

"Never better," Beck responded, and she meant it.

Grammy gave her an inquisitive look. "If you say so. Here." She pushed the tray of drinks toward Beck. "Take these to the girls over there."

The bookstore stayed busy for the next hour as several more groups of sunbathers stopped in for a cold drink after their day at the beach. A few ordered a sandwich or a scone.

When they closed for the day at six o'clock and were tidying up the kitchen, Beck asked her grandmother, "What would you think about inviting Joe and Lisa Davidson over tomorrow night for dinner? They might like a home-cooked meal and some company?"

Grammy raised her eyebrows in surprise but seemed pleased with the idea. "I think that's a wonderful idea. How nice of you to think of them." But she eyed her granddaughter suspiciously. "I sense, though, that this sudden idea isn't just out of the kindness of your heart?"

Beck gave her grandmother a sideways smile. "Why Grammy? What makes you think I have ulterior motives?"

"I'm not quite sure," her grandmother answered, eyeing her closely. "I'm just noticing a change in attitude. What's going on?"

Beck knew she couldn't get anything past her grandmother. "Well, you remember how growing up, I always wanted to be a detective?"

Her grandmother tilted her white-haired head and focused an incredulous stare at Beck as if she couldn't believe she was asking the question. "Remember? That was all you talked about for years."

Beck nodded. "Well, as you know, I never followed through with going into law enforcement—professionally, I mean. But I've decided to do some sleuthing into who killed Peggy Davidson."

"Really?" Grammy answered, a gleam entering her eyes. "Now that sounds interesting."

"But, Grammy, I'm doing this on my own. I'm not letting the police know I'm doing it or they'll tell me not to."

Her grandmother seemed unsure. "Not even Devon?"

"Especially not Devon," Beck responded. She'd never told her mother or grandmother about her unpleasant college experience, and she didn't plan to now. Her mother, Beck sensed, had been happy when she switched majors because she thought law enforcement was too dangerous a field for her daughter.

"I know you're crazy about Devon, Grammy, but this is something I want to do myself. Just a little investigating on my own."

Her grandmother reached up and took her by the shoulders, her alert blue eyes staring directly into Beck's.

"I do like Devon, Beck, but you're my granddaughter and I like you a lot more. If this is something you want to do, if this is something that will make you happy, I think it's great. Just so long as it's not dangerous."

Beck shook her head and assured her grandmother there was no danger involved. "I just think the police are really off base looking so closely at Scratchoff. And maybe Lydia and Phil, too, although I'm sure you'd be thrilled if it turned out to be them."

Miss Alice gave her a sly smile. "That's probably true, but I agree with you. Scratchoff is annoying as all get-out, but he's harmless. We've known him for years, so we know what he's like. Devon's new in town, so he doesn't understand."

Beck nodded, in complete agreement with her grandmother.

"My thought, Grammy, is to learn everything I can about Peggy Davidson. I think this murder might be more about someone who wanted to be sure she was dead than it is about that ring."

Her grandmother's eyes lit up as she got the intent of Beck's words. "So, you want to invite the Davidsons over so we can grill them?"

Beck chuckled. "Well, not exactly grill them," she replied. "Especially since they're still grieving. I just want to find out more about Peggy, if she had any enemies, if there's anyone who might be here in town who might want to see her dead."

Grammy rubbed her hands together with glee. "We'll double team them. They'll never know what hit them," she said, adding sheepishly, "But, of course, we'll kill them with kindness at the same time."

"I like the way you think, Grammy."

Her grandmother seemed very pleased with that comment.

"I'm so glad you want to help me, Grammy. It means a lot to me, and I can really use the assistance."

"I'll be your Watson, Sherlock."

Beck flashed her a wide smile. "I like that idea!"

"What do you want me to do first?" her grandmother asked.

"Why don't you invite them, Grammy? That would seem more natural."

"I'll be happy too. I'll do that as soon as we get done here." She opened the refrigerator to put in a plateful of sandwiches bundled in plastic wrap. "Now the important part. What should we cook for dinner?"

"You know what I'd like," Beck told her grandmother with a grin. "Your specialty."

"Let's see," Grammy teased, "could it be grouper in caper sauce and lemon rice? Maybe a little broccoli in garlic butter on the side?"

"I can't think of anything better. Just thinking about it makes me hungry."

"What about dessert?" Grammy asked.

"I have a new recipe for key lime pie that I've been dying to try," Beck said.

"Can't wait to taste it," Grammy said. She looked thoughtful for a moment and then added, "I think we might want to get a big jug of pinot grigio wine, too. That might loosen their lips a little bit."

"Grammy!"

"And, to be kind, it'll make them forget their troubles for a little while," her grandmother added coyly with an impish grin.

Beck never knew what was going to come out of her grandmother's mouth. But she liked the idea of the wine. She didn't drink much or often, but a nice glass of white wine with a good seafood dinner was a treat.

When they went upstairs, Beck heard Grammy on the phone with Lisa Davidson. A few minutes later, she popped her head in Beck's room. "We're on for dinner. The game is afoot."

Beck laughed at the Sherlock Holmes reference. Grammy would be an excellent Watson.

"Oh," her grandmother added, "Lisa's brother is in town visiting them. He's coming, too."

"Hmmm," Beck thought. "Should be an interesting dinner."

Chapter Eighteen

Beck asked Lizzie if she would like to come to dinner with the Davidsons, but to her relief, Lizzie turned her down. Lizzie seemed less than enthused about the idea of spending the evening with a grieving couple from North Carolina and was quick to let Beck know she already had other plans. She and Teddy were going out for pizza and a movie. Beck was relieved because she wanted to have an uninterrupted conversation with the victim's son and daughter-in-law.

Mid-morning after the breakfast crowd left, Beck drove to the grocery store up the beach to buy the ingredients they would need to make dinner for their guests that night. When she arrived back at the bookstore with her arms full of grocery bags, she found Dorothy sitting at the counter sipping coffee and talking with her grandmother. Of course, her poodle Fifi was nosing around the bookstore's kitchen floor and her baby carriage was parked in the corner.

"Hi, Dorothy," Beck called out as she climbed the stairs to their apartment kitchen, juggling five bags at once so she'd only have to make one trip up the stairs.

"Hello, dear. Careful there," the older woman answered, not missing a beat in her conversation with Beck's grandmother.

It took Beck ten minutes to unload all of her purchases before she headed back downstairs. The two white-haired ladies were deep in conversation about which college Dorothy's granddaughter should attend. The girl was leaning toward an expensive private school out of state, but Dorothy thought she should go to a state university in Florida to get the same or better education for a much lower price.

"Of course, it's not my decision," she was saying, "but I hate to see my son footing the bill after he's been contributing all these years to the prepaid in-state tuition program."

Dorothy came up for a breath and turned her attention toward Beck. "What do you think, Beck?"

"Oh." Caught off-guard, Beck tried to think as she stepped behind the cash register. "Well, let's see. I'm very pleased with the education I got at a state college. I'm sure I could have spent thousands more at a private school for a similar education and would still be paying off college loans."

"There, see?" Dorothy told Grammy. "I told you so."

"Hey," Grammy said, raising her hands in rebuttal. "You're preaching to the choir."

Her grandmother turned toward Beck. "Speaking of your college days, Beck, Dorothy had a visit from your old classmate, Devon."

"Detective Mathis? I sure did." Dorothy picked up Fifi and gave her a cuddle. "That is one handsome man. And single, too, it looks like. If I were younger—"

Grammy sighed. "You and me both."

Beck flashed an amused smile at the two women and shook her head. "Oh, c'mon. You both were very happily married for over forty years."

The elderly women looked at each other and their faces crinkled into mischievous grins.

"Doesn't mean we can't appreciate a little eye candy every now and then," Dorothy said.

"That's for darn sure," Grammy agreed, with a glint in her eye.

Beck laughed. "You two."

"What about you, Beck?" Dorothy urged. "You ought to grab him before somebody else does."

"Yeah," Grammy agreed, her face lighting up as if it were the first time she'd thought of it. "Sure would be nice to have him in the family."

Beck shook her head, her last conversation with Devon still very much in her mind. "No, thank you. Not interested. I have more than enough to keep me busy here at the bookstore."

Not in the mood for a matchmaking session, Beck quickly changed the subject. "So, what did the detective want to know, Dorothy?"

"Mainly just what the woman who got killed and I talked about." She added proudly. "I'm kind of a witness."

Beck was half surprised he hadn't accused her of being the murderer, too.

"What did you tell him?" she asked.

Dorothy cleared her throat, obviously enjoying being the center of attention.

"Just that she was excited to talk to the author because they went to high school together. I asked her if they were close friends, but she said they weren't. She couldn't remember exactly how she knew her, if they had classes together or what, because it was nearly fifty years ago. But, for whatever reason, she remembered her real well."

"Anything else?" Beck prompted. She wanted to find out as much as she could about the murder from every source she could.

Fifi started to squirm in Dorothy's arms, so she set her down on the floor. The poodle immediately ran behind the counter to join Coquina in the kitchen.

"Well," Dorothy answered, "he asked me about her showing off her ring and who else had noticed."

"What'd you say?"

"The people sitting on the other side of her were real interested. I don't know them, but I picked up that they own the jewelry store next door. They were asking her all kinds of questions about the ring. Then there was a real estate lady sitting next to me who was looking at it, too. Lucy something."

"That's Lucy Granger," Grammy interjected. "She leaves her business cards here to try to pick up clients. I don't think she gets too many. Doesn't have the personality for sales, if you know what I mean."

Beck laughed. "Like you, you mean?"

Grammy nodded and reached out both of her arms as if she were driving a car. "Exactly. You've gotta put your foot on the gas and not let up."

Dorothy giggled. "You've definitely got that one down, Alice."

Beck chuckled, too, and then returned her attention to Dorothy.

"Was there anybody else who seemed particularly interested in Peggy Davidson or her emerald ring?"

"I told the detective that Scratchoff McLean kept peeking over my shoulder to get a look at it. That man can be so annoying."

"Tell me about it," Grammy huffed. "Just be glad you don't own a store open to the public where he can come in any time he darn well pleases. He's in here at least three or four times a week."

Dorothy shook her head in sympathy. "I sure do pity you there."

"Anybody else?" Beck asked. "Or did you talk to anyone else after the book signing?"

Dorothy shook her head. “No, that was about it. After I got my book signed, I didn’t stay around. It was getting to be my bedtime, so I went upstairs and got Fifi and then left.”

Her grandmother’s friend stepped down from the counter stool and glanced around for her dog.

“Fifi, c’mon girl. Time to go home.” She walked to the corner where the baby carriage was parked and pushed it toward the kitchen. “Jerome should be finished mowing my yard by now. Fifi barks her head off when he’s mowing, so it’s best I get her out of the house.”

Finding the dog curled up next to Coquina, Dorothy picked her up and settled her into the baby carriage. “I’ll see you ladies later,” she said, pushing the carriage to the front door. “Stay safe and lock your doors.”

“You too, Dorothy,” Grammy called out to her. “Don’t be a stranger.”

Chapter Nineteen

Beck spread her mother's delicate lace tablecloth over the mahogany table and took their best china out of the dining room hutch. She'd already dressed for dinner, choosing a flowered silk blouse and a pair of pale yellow slacks. As she started setting the table, Lizzie appeared, stared at the table, and frowned at her sister.

"Why so fancy shmancy? This looks like Christmas or something."

Beck didn't miss a beat in setting the cutlery. "We want this to be an extra nice dinner," she answered, not looking up. She moved around the table to the next setting. "These people just had a traumatic death in their family, so we want to make this dinner special for them."

"That's nice, I guess," Lizzie replied, a perplexed look on her face. "But why do you have to do it?"

Beck looked up at her sister, not hiding her surprise at the question.

"Lizzie! Because their mother spent the last hour of her life in our bookstore, and when she left, she was murdered."

Lizzie shrugged. "Oh. Okay. I guess."

Her cell phone rang. "Hi, Teddy." She turned to walk down the hall. "What time are you coming to pick me up?"

Beck reached into the hutch again and took out their best crystal wine glasses. She heard Lizzie say, "Good. I want to get out of here before those relatives of that dead lady get here. Beck and Grammy invited them over for dinner."

Beck sighed. Empathy apparently wasn't a strong point yet in her nineteen-year-old sister's brain. A few minutes later, Lizzie appeared dressed in jeans and a halter top, her purse slung over her shoulder.

"Leaving already?" Beck asked.

"Yeah. Teddy wants me to pick him up. His car's been acting up." She gave the table another puzzled look. "Have fun. I guess."

When she turned to go, Beck decided to confide in her.

"I know you think it's weird us going to all this trouble, but I have another reason for inviting the Davidsons to dinner."

Lizzie's interest was piqued. "Really?" She sat down in a dining room chair. "What?"

Beck felt the excitement growing within her. Every time she thought about actually investigating a crime, she felt a thrill.

"Remember how I told you I always wanted to be a detective?"

Lizzie nodded and leaned forward with interest.

"Well, I'm going to do some investigating of my own into this murder. And my first step is to interview the family to learn as much as I can about the victim."

"Really? That's so cool! It would be great if you figured it out before the police do. Now I kinda wish I could come to the dinner, too, so I could watch."

Beck shook her head. "No, no. You already have plans and, besides, I don't want to overwhelm them. We're going to be very subtle. I don't want them to feel like they're being grilled. And we are doing this, too, to support them. I'm sure it can't be fun having to stay in a hotel for a week waiting for your mother's body to be released."

Lizzie scrunched her nose. "Yeah, that must be awful. But you have to tell me everything afterward. Okay? This is kind of exciting!"

They heard Grammy coming up the stairs after closing up the bookshop. It was just after six o'clock, and their guests would be arriving at seven.

Beck nodded. "I will. I promise."

Lizzie stood up and reached the stairs just as Grammy stepped onto the landing.

"Have a fun dinner, Grammy," Lizzie said, as she sailed past.

Grammy stopped and peered down the stairs after her granddaughter. "Where are you off to?"

Lizzie stopped at the bottom of the stairs and turned around. "Pizza and a movie. The new Star Wars."

"With Teddy?"

"Yes, Grammy." Beck noted a tone of resentment. Lizzie hated for her activities to be monitored. Nineteen was a tough age.

"Okay, have fun. Try not to be too late."

"Yes, Grammy," Lizzie replied in the same monotone. A couple of seconds later the front door slammed shut.

Beck gave her grandmother an amused look. "Teenage years are so much fun, aren't they?"

Grammy was blasé. "Nothing I can't handle. As long as she's living under this roof, she has to let her old grandmother know where she is and what she's doing. Your mother made me promise her that."

Beck thought of herself at nineteen. A freshman living on a college campus, she had all the freedom in the world, but she didn't take advantage of it. She was shy and studious, didn't date, and the most fun she had was an occasional pizza party with the girls in her dorm. She and Lizzie couldn't have been more different.

"The table looks wonderful," Grammy said, breaking Beck's reverie.

"Thank you," Beck responded, pleased. Her grandmother was usually a little stingy with compliments, so she savored any that she received.

"I'm going to get changed and then start dinner," Grammy said, heading for her bedroom.

"I'll be your sous chef," Beck told her. "Just let me know anything you need me to do."

"Sous chef?" Her grandmother chuckled. "I like the sound of that! Did you learn that on one of your fancy cooking shows?"

Actually, she did. Beck wasn't much of a cook herself but, for some reason, she relished watching cooking shows on television. Maybe because the meals they were able to prepare so quickly seemed like such an amazing feat to her. She was excited to watch her grandmother prepare the grouper dinner. But even more than that, she was eager to learn everything she could about Peggy Davidson's life from their guests.

Chapter Twenty

They kept the conversation light at the beginning of the dinner, talking about the weather, the beach, shopping, and books. Joe, not surprisingly, was somewhat somber but was polite to a fault and had an easy dignity about him. Lisa had a breezy personality and kept the conversation flowing with Beck and her grandmother. Looking tanned and beautiful, Lisa had dressed fashionably in an off-the-shoulder black-and-white striped top, tight-fitting white capri pants, and black heels.

Lisa's brother, Eric, a husky, fair-haired man who looked younger than his sister, ate more than he talked, but they learned he had recently moved to Ft. Lauderdale, a little over an hour south of Manatee Beach. Single, he seemed to be at loose ends and was job searching in South

Florida. He had a couple of interviews set up locally and was staying for a few days with the Davidsons at their hotel down the street.

Grammy, dressed in her usual dark pants but paired tonight with a flattering white tunic top, kept the white wine flowing. After they'd eaten the last of the grouper—which was a big hit with their guests—she refilled their wine glasses and then raised hers in a toast to the recently departed Peggy Davidson.

"To Peggy," Grammy toasted. "May she rest in peace."

"Amen," her son said, raising his glass. "To the best mother a person could have."

They all toasted and took a drink of wine.

"Tell us about your mother, Joe," Grammy said, taking the lead, to Beck's relief. "She seemed like such a nice woman. Where did she grow up?"

Joe leaned back in his chair and contemplated for a moment. "My mother's family lived in the Research Triangle area of North Carolina, outside of Raleigh. Her father was a physician who did some groundbreaking research in the area of brain stem injuries. Dr. Dennis Hinson. He's very well known in medical circles."

"Wow," Beck interjected. "How impressive."

Joe nodded. "So, my mother had a pretty privileged upbringing. You know the south back then, cotillions, coming out parties, the whole bit."

Beck noticed a surreptitious glance pass between Lisa Davidson and her brother. But it disappeared as quickly as it happened, and the frozen smile returned that had been planted on Lisa's face since her husband began speaking about his mother.

"You wouldn't know it by looking at her now." He stopped and choked up a little. "I mean in her later years. But in high school, she played tennis and was on the high school team. I don't think she played much after that, though. I never saw her play."

His mention of high school brought up one of the main questions Beck wanted answered that night.

"Where did your mother go to high school, Joe? I'm curious because she and the author at the book signing went to high school together. Was it a private school?"

Joe eyed her with interest. "That's right. I remember Mom saying that." He stopped to take a sip of water. "No, surprisingly with their background, she didn't go to a private school. Apparently my grandfather was adamant about that because the public schools around there were very good because it was a medical community. She went to Deerwood High."

Beck noticed Lisa's brother Eric frown a bit, but he didn't say anything. He took a big gulp of wine, and Grammy refilled his glass. No one was driving, thank goodness, Beck realized, because if she counted right, he was on number four. She was just midway through her second glass and already feeling it.

"How did your parents meet, Joe?" Grammy asked.

"They both went to Duke and met each other their first day on campus freshman year." His face lit up as he described it. "They always said it was love at first sight."

"Kind of like us," Lisa said, squeezing his hand. He nodded and squeezed her hand back.

"A lot like us," Joe told them, still gazing at his wife. "Lisa and I were married six months after we met. Just had our first anniversary last month."

Sounds pretty whirlwind, Beck thought, a little surprised at how quickly they married.

"And how did the two of you meet?" Grammy asked. "College, too?"

"Oh, no," Joe chuckled. "I was out playing golf at one of the big resorts up in the Outer Banks, and Lisa waited on us in the cocktail lounge afterward. Like she said, it was love at first sight."

Lisa colored a little. "It was just a summer job for me."

Joe continued, "Then, I very slyly got her a job as a receptionist in my father's company so I could see her every day."

"Your father's company?" Beck asked

"Yes, my dad, Joe, Sr., was an engineer who started his own company with a friend of his from Duke. And, of course, he guided my career path that way, too. I also got my engineering degree from Duke."

"How nice that you and your father got to work together," Grammy chimed in. "There's nothing like a family business, right Beck?"

Beck smiled. "It definitely has its benefits. But I'm sure our little bookstore doesn't compare to Joe's family business."

The look on Lisa's face told them, "Not by a long shot."

"My father was a workaholic," Joe said. "He worked twenty-four/seven to build that business. I barely saw him growing up, but their engineering firm became one of the largest in the South with over thirty branch offices."

"My goodness," Grammy exclaimed. "Thirty branches! Isn't that something."

"That's really impressive," Beck agreed. "But it must have been kind of hard on your mother with your dad being at work all the time." She realized she was projecting how she would have felt if she were in that situation.

"It was, I think," Joe replied. "But besides taking care of me, she kind of threw herself into charity work. It seemed like she was on every board in town."

"Was that in the Outer Banks?" Beck asked. "I remember you saying that's where you're from."

"Yes," Joe answered, glancing at Grammy. "Not too far from Kitty Hawk, you remember, the Wright Brothers and all that?"

Grammy feigned displeasure. "Well, young man, I remember from the history books, but I'm not that old!"

That brought a laugh from everyone at the table.

"But after Joe and I got married, we moved down to the Hatteras area," Lisa said. "It's a couple of hours south."

"Don't want to be too close to the in-laws, right, Sis?" Eric said, inappropriately. Lisa shot her brother a disapproving look before continuing.

"The islands are all so beautiful. A lot like here," Lisa described. "Gorgeous wide beaches, lots of surfing, quaint homes and inns, and wonderful restaurants. Of course, the weather in the winter isn't nearly as warm as here, so summer is the high season up there."

"And don't forget the hurricanes!" Joe said. "We've had our fill of those. My parents had to rebuild twice. That's why we're thinking of moving down here."

Beck remembered another question she wanted to be sure to ask. "Did your mother have friends who live down here?"

"Actually, my mother's best friend, going all the way back to high school, lives in Palm Beach. Lenora Palmer. She's my godmother. Maybe you've heard of her husband, Jordan Palmer, the developer? He's the one who's building SeaBreeze Point north of Manatee Beach."

The name did ring a bell. Beck thought she recalled reading about him in the newspaper. He developed high-end resorts and was building a large resort community on undeveloped beachfront north of Manatee Beach. The development had created a lot of controversy in town, both with the residents and the city council. Grammy had been very vocal about her disapproval of the development. Beck sent her a warning look that said, "Not now."

Grammy's eyes flashed, and it was obvious to Beck she was biting her lip. Hard. Beck was surprised and relieved when her grandmother didn't bring up the community's opposition to the project, but instead said to Joe, "They went to high school together? That is indeed a long friendship."

"We just visited them the day before—" Joe looked like he might choke up again. "I called them to tell them what happened."

Beck could see he needed a moment so she directed a question to Lisa.

"Since you're considering moving down to Florida, do you know anyone else down here?"

"I don't," Lisa responded. "But I love meeting new people, so it would be an adventure."

"I have a couple of college friends down in Miami," Joe added. "But that's about it. We'd pretty much be starting over socially."

Beck turned her attention to Eric.

"And you've moved to Ft. Lauderdale, Eric? How do you like it?"

Eric wiped his mouth with a napkin, nodding while he did it. "I like it a lot. Just hope I'm able to find a job down there."

"What kind of work do you do, Eric?" Grammy asked.

"Oh, a little bit of this, a little bit of that. Mainly construction."

"Well, there's definitely a lot of construction going on down in Ft. Lauderdale and Miami," Grammy replied. "Just hope it stays down there. We like our little town exactly like it is."

"I don't blame you there," Lisa said. "This is a lovely area. I could see us living here."

"Well, we would love to see you move here," Grammy said, bringing her forefinger to her lips. "Just don't tell anyone else about our little piece of paradise."

"Mum's the word," Joe promised with a sly smile.

It was starting to get late, and after all the wine they'd drunk, it was time for some coffee.

"I hope you saved room for my homemade key lime pie," Beck said to them, as she started to clear the table.

Eric's eyes lit up. "That sounds great. My favorite kind of pie."

"Mine too," Joe said, standing up. "I'd like to wash up if you don't mind."

Beck pointed the way to the bathroom, and Lisa stood up and began collecting dirty dishes to take into the kitchen.

"Now, now. You're our guest," Grammy told her. "You sit down and chat with your brother. We'll take care of this."

When they went into the kitchen, Coquina got to her feet and her nose went into the air, sniffing. She'd been trained not to beg at the table, and she often stayed in the kitchen at dinner time. She didn't beg, but anything that hit the floor was hers, and she'd learned that if she was patient while they ate, some dinner scraps would likely be coming her way. And that was the case tonight. Grammy scraped a few pieces of uneaten fish and rice into the dog's bowl.

While Beck and her grandmother cleaned up the dishes and prepared the pie and coffee, Beck kept a sharp ear open to the conversation at the dining room table.

While Joe was in the bathroom, she heard Eric say to Lisa, "They sure were asking a lot of personal questions."

"Probably just nosy," she heard Lisa reply. "You know how these small towns are."

"Yeah, I guess a murder like this is the most excitement they ever see."

"Eric!" she chastised him. "Would you watch what you say?"

Joe returned from the bathroom just as Grammy entered the room carrying a tray of coffee cups and a coffee pot.

Beck served her key lime pie and was thrilled that it came out even better than she'd expected. The men were so complimentary that she wrapped up the rest of the pie for them to take back to the hotel.

When it was time to leave, all three dinner guests said how much they had enjoyed the evening. And Joe was especially appreciative.

"I can't tell you how much it meant to me to be able to talk about my mother tonight," he told them as they said goodbye at the door. "I've been holding in so much, that just remembering the good times helps. Thank you for taking such an interest."

Grammy took hold of his hands. “I’m so glad we could help. Remember, you can call on us anytime. We’re here for you.”

Chapter Twenty-One

"I think that went well all the way around," Beck told her grandmother after their guests left. "They seemed to genuinely enjoy the evening and talking about his mother seemed cathartic for Joe. And, from our point of view, we learned a lot of valuable information."

Grammy agreed and was especially pleased with Joe's last comments to them. "I'm just so glad we could do a little bit to make him feel better."

"I know," Beck said. "I'm still having trouble getting past the fact that his poor mother died after leaving our bookstore. Anything we can do to make them feel better, makes me feel better, too."

Grammy poured herself a cup of decaf coffee and asked Beck if she wanted one.

"If I have one more drink of anything, I'm going to float away," Beck said, adding, "I'll be right back."

She went to her bedroom, rummaged through a desk drawer, and pulled out a yellow legal pad. She grabbed a pen from the desk and took them to the dining room table.

"Okay," Beck said, sitting down. "I'm going to make a list of things we learned tonight and things we need to look into. That's the way to stay organized."

Grammy sat down in a dining room chair next to her and stirred her coffee. "What first?" she asked.

"First, I'm going to make a list of everything we know about Peggy Davidson's life now that we didn't know before."

"Okay, shoot," Grammy said, looking at Beck expectantly.

"Number one," Beck said, writing on the notepad as she spoke, under a headline: Peggy Davidson's Background. "Peggy Davidson grew up in the Research Triangle of North Carolina, the daughter of privilege. Her father was a well-known doctor."

"Anything else?" she asked her grandmother.

"Not really. Just the specifics that she went to cotillions, had a debutante party, played tennis."

"Right. Okay, number two. She went to—" Beck suddenly had trouble remembering the name of the high school she attended. Maybe the wine was clouding her memory. And that had been one of the main pieces of information she'd wanted to learn that evening.

"Deerwood High School," her grandmother provided. Thank God for Grammy's memory, Beck thought. Like an elephant.

"It was a public high school," her grandmother continued. "Her father wanted her to go to a public high school instead of a private one because the schools up there were good because of all the doctors and scientists in the area."

"And that's where she met Marcia Graybill," Beck interjected. "And that's one thing we really want to look into. Peggy told Dorothy they weren't close, but she distinctly remembers her for some reason. She just couldn't remember exactly what. We'll definitely follow up on that."

"And," Grammy reminded her, "Peggy's best friend Lenora Palmer also went to high school with them. She lives in Palm Beach now with her husband who's the developer of SeaBreeze Point."

Grammy rubbed her thumb and fingers together. "Palm Beach. Not just anybody can afford to live in Palm Beach."

"That's for sure," Beck agreed, not looking up for the long list she was writing.

"Let me do the next one," Grammy offered. "Number three. Peggy went to Duke University where she met her husband, Joe Davidson, Sr., on the first day of their freshman year. After they were married they moved to the Outer Banks of North Carolina, the northern part, near Kitty Hawk."

Beck nodded as she continued to write on the legal pad.

"Number four," Beck said, taking over the summary, "Her husband built an extremely successful engineering firm that made them very wealthy. It has thirty branches around the South. Her husband worked all the time, and Peggy got involved in volunteer work. She served on a number of boards in the area and was very well known for her volunteer work."

"Number five," Grammy said, taking her turn. "Her only son, Joe, got married a year ago to a woman who was working as a cocktail waitress at the club where he played golf."

They both stopped and looked at each other. Beck raised an eyebrow. “That doesn’t sound too good on paper, does it?” she asked, as she jotted it down.

“No, it doesn’t,” Grammy answered. “An incredibly wealthy man marries a cocktail waitress after knowing her for only six months.”

She paused. “Of course, you never know. Love is a crazy thing.”

“True,” Beck agreed. “And she is a strikingly beautiful woman. She looked gorgeous tonight in that outfit. I can see how he would be immediately interested in her.”

“Her brother was a little rough around the edges,” Grammy said, giving Beck a questioning look. “Nothing like Joe.”

“Not at all,” Beck agreed. “That’s another angle we need to look at closely. Checking into her brother’s background.”

Beck drew a bold line across the middle of the page and wrote another subhead: Information Gathering.

Her grandmother released a long sigh. “That’s a lot. Where do we start?”

“The first thing I want to know,” Beck said, “that’s been bothering me all along, is why Marcia Graybill reacted so negatively to Peggy. What could have happened in high school nearly fifty years ago that still would bring such a negative reaction?"

Grammy shrugged. "I guess it could have been a lot of things. High school isn't always fun, and the memories can be etched on your brain for life."

"Very true," Beck replied, as a few unpleasant teenage memories flitted through her brain. She pushed them aside. She didn't have time to go down memory lane right now.

"How are you going to find out?" Grammy asked, perplexed about how to start.

"I'd been thinking about an online service where you can get yearbooks from years ago. But after dinner tonight, I'm hoping to find out what I need to know a much easier way. I'm going to pay Peggy Davidson's best friend from high school a visit down in Palm Beach. I filed away her name in my mind when Joe said it. Lenora Palmer. And her husband is that well-known developer Jordan Palmer."

"Maybe she'll remember the author and be able to tell you about her," Grammy said, adding, "And while you're there, give them my two cents about what I think about that development of theirs!"

"I'm not going to do that, Grammy."

"Maybe I should come along?" she said in jest.

"No," Beck chuckled. "This is not the time for you to get on your bandwagon. Anyway, somebody needs to tend the store."

Grammy shrugged. "Okay, okay. I hope she remembers Marcia Graybill."

"Even if she doesn't, hopefully she will have a yearbook that I can look at."

"A yearbook? Will that tell much?" Grammy asked.

"I may be able to pick up some useful information there. Photos might give me some leads to other friends who might know more."

Beck listed another subhead under Information Gathering: Marcia Graybill. Then she wrote: talk to Lenora Palmer, obtain yearbook, possibly talk to other old friends, talk to the author, talk to her husband.

"I want to talk to the author's husband to find out what they were having such a long conversation about," Beck said. "But I'd rather wait to talk to him until after I know more about the two women's high school relationship."

"What next?" Grammy asked, obviously excited to be part of the investigation.

“We also need to gather information about Peggy’s life up in the Outer Banks, what her friends have to say about her, and particularly, how she and her daughter-in-law got along. As well as information about her brother, Eric.”

“How will we do that?” Grammy asked.

“I have an idea about that. Obviously, I’ll Google her first to see what’s out there on her and, hopefully, there may be some pictures of her at events. Then, I’ll go online to look at the society pages of the newspaper up there. I’ll bet I’ll come across quite a bit if she’s that active. If I’m able to get some names of her friends, we can make some phone calls.”

“And Lenora Palmer might know some people who are close to her up there, too,” Grammy suggested. “Friends usually know who other friends are.”

“I like that,” Beck said. “I knew you’d be good at this, Grammy. Or should I say Watson?”

Grammy obviously liked the comment. Beck gave her grandmother a serious stare. “I just know, Grammy, the more we learn about Peggy Davidson’s life, the closer we’ll get to figuring out who wanted her dead.”

Beck held up her hand for a high five. Grammy slapped it. “We’re going to make a great team!”

Chapter Twenty-Two

Beck was anxious to get started the next morning, but she needed Lenora Palmer's phone number. She was trying to think of how to approach Joe Davidson for it, when the phone rang. It was Joe.

"I just wanted to call to thank you so much for the nice dinner last night," he said. "Like I was telling you and your grandmother last night, it was just the medicine I needed to help me feel better. We have to wait so long for her funeral, that it was cathartic for me to be able to talk about her for an evening."

Beck's heart went out to him. "I'm so happy we were able to help," she told him sincerely. "We both really enjoyed the evening, too. You know, the fact that your mother spent time in our store on her last night had a big impact on us. We want to do anything we can to help."

"Well, we all had a good time. I know Lisa and Eric both said they enjoyed the dinner, too."

She could tell he was about to hang up when she decided to go out on a limb and ask him for his mother's friend's phone number.

"Oh, Joe," she said as if she'd just thought of it. "I have to be down in Palm Beach tomorrow, and I thought that maybe while I'm there, I could drop by to offer my condolences to your godmother, Lenora Palmer. Like I said, your mother's death hit my grandmother and me hard, and it would mean a lot to me to be able to tell your mother's best friend how sorry we are."

Joe didn't reply right away, and she thought she might have overstepped her bounds. She knew it was a stretch, but she really wanted to talk to Lenora Palmer. It was the only excuse she could think of. But after a few moments, Joe thanked her for the thought and kindly offered to phone his godmother to set up a meeting. He had such good manners and such a nice way about him. Peggy must have been so proud about what a fine man he had become.

He asked Beck what time would be good for her, and she told him anytime in the afternoon that was convenient for his godmother. He told her he would make the call and get back to her.

Ten minutes later, Beck's phone rang. Joe told her his godmother Lenora would be expecting her at three o'clock the next day and gave her the address. It would have been nice to take Grammy along on the visit, too, but somebody had to run the store. The three o'clock meeting time would be perfect. She'd be able to help Grammy with lunch and then leave about two o'clock for the drive south.

Lizzie appeared at her sister's bedroom door. "How did it go last night? Did you find out anything important?"

Beck caught her up on the dinner conversation and told her about her scheduled visit the next day to see Peggy Davidson's best friend in Palm Beach.

"You're finding out so much! You're really good at this."

The compliment made Beck feel good. She did feel like she was on to something and having Lizzie's encouragement felt great.

"And you know the best thing?" Lizzie asked.

"What?" Beck was curious for her sister's viewpoint.

"When you solve this before the police do, you're really going to get Devon's attention."

Beck sighed and frowned at her sister. "That is not what this is all about, Lizzie. I'm doing this because it's my passion and I'm good at it, not to get a man's attention. And I want to find out what really happened to that poor woman when she left our store."

"I know, I know," Lizzie told her. "But a side benefit is that you will impress Devon. Men act like they don't like it when a woman beats them at something, but down deep they do. The ones worth anything, anyway. Then you're a challenge to them."

Beck wondered if that was really true. She wasn't athletic, so she'd never really had the experience of beating a man at much of anything, except maybe a grade in school. She did remember beating her old boyfriend Darren at Scrabble a few times, and he didn't seem to like it. She recalled letting him win the last time they played.

But Lizzie excelled at every sport she'd ever tried, from swimming to softball to tennis. And she relished rubbing it in when she beat the boys. It never seemed to keep any of them away. In fact, it seemed to draw them to her. So maybe she had something there.

"So, do you beat Teddy at sports?" Beck asked her sister.

Lizzie shrugged. "We haven't really played any. He's a great surfer, so that's cool. I'm not nearly as good as he is. Maybe I'll challenge him to a tennis game one of these days. Gotta keep him in his place."

How her nineteen-year-old sister was able to manage men so better than she did, was beyond her. Not that men were at the top of her priority list right now. She had a murder she wanted to solve. And whether she impressed Devon Mathis or not, wasn't even on her radar.

That night Beck spent a couple of hours on her computer Googling Peggy Davidson and her family. She found numerous entries and photos of Peggy, attending this garden club or that charitable event in various Outer Banks communities. Her son wasn't kidding when he said she seemed to be involved in every volunteer group around. Besides that, Beck came across her husband's lengthy obituary, which included a lot of the information Joe had talked about at dinner. She also found several announcements on Joe, about what you'd expect from a prominent family—his acceptance to Duke, his graduation from Duke, his signing on with his father's engineering firm, and then his being made partner.

But news articles she expected to find that seemed to be missing were Joe and Lisa's engagement and wedding announcements. Given the family's social standing, Beck expected to see detailed articles and large photos of the happy couple. Instead, all she could find was a small announcement of Joe and Lisa's wedding that merely said the couple had been married in a private destination wedding in Hawaii. There wasn't even a photo with it. She was able to learn from the short article that Lisa's maiden name was Jones. Great, Beck thought. Lisa Jones and Eric Jones. That would make the search into their backgrounds a lot more complicated. She closed her laptop with a sigh. She was tired and that search would have to wait until tomorrow.

Chapter Twenty-Three

Beck pulled out of the carport behind the bookshop in her white mini-Cooper convertible, one of the rare splurges she'd made when she decided to settle in the seaside community where she grew up. The car sometimes sat for a week at a time without being driven since her commute to work consisted of approximately twenty steps down the stairs. Other than an occasional trip to the grocery store, everything else in her life was within walking distance—the beach, the gym, clothing shops, and her favorite restaurants.

So, she looked forward to her short road trip south to Palm Beach to visit Peggy Davidson's best friend, Lenora Palmer. With a blue cloudless sky above, the warm rays of the sun beating down, and her hair blowing wildly in the wind, she flew down A1A in her little convertible. Being a weekday, the road wasn't busy and the beaches in uninhabited areas were nearly deserted. The ocean was glassy and a deep aqua blue, and she followed its path until the road curved inland. Forty-five minutes later, she was crossing the Intracoastal Waterway bridge from West Palm Beach to the millionaire's enclave of Palm Beach. The mansions, past and present, of such well-known families as the Kennedys, the Trumps, the Kochs, Estee Lauder, James Patterson, and many others stood behind walls of impeccably manicured hedges offering various levels of seclusion. Their yachts dotted the harbor. The landscaping in this town was incredible. Beck decided a good gardener could probably earn enough money to eventually buy one of these homes someday.

Beck arrived a little early, so she decided to take a little tour around the wealthy island community. She passed by The Breakers historic hotel and its impressive lawns, built by Henry Flagler in the early 1900s, and Mar-a-Lago, the palatial mansion originally built by E.F. Hutton and his wife Marjorie Merriweather Post that later became the home of President Donald Trump. Checking the address Joe had given her for Lenora Palmer's home, she drove down Ocean Avenue past the high hedges of the former Kennedy compound and other estates until she saw the open gate of the Palmer's huge, oceanfront mansion.

Turning in, Beck drove up the long stone driveway that was lined by dozens of magnificent royal palms. She gasped as she got her first view of the Palmer's huge Mediterranean-style home with its red-tile roof and huge terrace across the front. It looked more like a hotel than a house. Beck pulled her car up next to the estate's four-car garage and turned off the ignition. Checking the mirror, she took a couple of minutes to brush her tangled hair into place, wishing for a moment that she'd followed her grandmother's advice to wear a scarf. But she hadn't been in the mood for that—she wanted the freedom of the wind in her hair. Her hair was pretty straight anyway, and she knew it would look acceptable enough if she had time to brush it out.

Flushed from the wind, her cheeks gave her face a healthy glow. She added a dab of lipstick and a quick couple of strokes of mascara before stepping out of the car. A slight breeze off the ocean ruffled the petals of the yellow hibiscus flowers on a hedge leading up to the house. She was surprised to see that the hedge, like the grass, was a little overgrown, and a few weeds crept out from beneath some of the stepping stones.

When Beck rang the doorbell, she thought she might be greeted by a tuxedoed butler or a uniformed maid, judging by the size of the estate. But a slim, blonde woman with sparkling blue eyes and a charming smile opened the door and introduced herself as Lenora Palmer. She wore a simple Lily Pulitzer flowered dress that complimented her figure and her tan. Beck found it difficult to believe this woman was the same age as Peggy Davidson.

Lenora was beyond gracious as Beck offered the Palm Beach woman her condolences at the front door. She then led Beck through the opulently furnished home to a sunroom at the back of the house. The view of the ocean through floor-to-ceiling glass panels was breathtaking. The long, marble-tiled sunroom overflowed with custom-designed rattan couches and settees, flowering South Florida plants in colorful urns, and so many hanging plants that the room could have doubled as a greenhouse. Lenora sat down on a long couch covered in a satin palm tree print and invited Beck to join her. A pitcher of iced tea with two tall glasses filled with ice and a small charcuterie board with a variety of cheeses sat on the coffee table in front of them. This woman certainly knew how to make a guest feel welcomed.

"I was very happy to hear from Joe that you wanted to pay me a visit," Lenora told her in an unexpectedly forthright fashion. "As you can imagine, my husband and I were both just stunned at what happened to Peggy, and Joe was certainly in no state to tell us much. My godson is so sensitive. This has hit him incredibly hard. I didn't want to ask him details because I knew it would be too painful for him."

Beck felt relieved that Peggy's best friend seemed so open and easy to talk to. Perhaps this discussion might not be as awkward as she had feared it might be.

"Please," Lenora said, "Tell me everything you know about the attack."

"Your friend was actually at the bookstore I own with my grandmother, attending a book signing, right before her death. She was killed walking back to the hotel afterward."

Beck hesitated and peered down at her hands. "This has hit my grandmother and me very deeply. We can't help feeling a degree of pain and guilt about her death."

Lenora grasped one of Beck's hands and covered it with her own. "Oh, my dear, you shouldn't," she said with a sincerity Beck rarely heard. "We live in a violent world, and we can't blame ourselves for criminal acts that are out of our control."

The woman's voice was so soothing, and Beck knew what she said held a degree of truth. But Beck had begun to realize that it would be a long time before she got over Peggy Davidson's death.

"Thank you," she told the older woman. "I appreciate your kind words."

Lenora patted her hand and took hers back, folding them in her lap. "Please tell me what you know about what happened to Peggy after she left your store. We've looked in the papers, but the police aren't saying much at all."

Beck certainly knew that was true. She'd been shocked at the small amount of detail the media had reported on the crime.

"From what I understand," Beck told her, "after Peggy left the bookstore, she only made it as far as the jewelry store next door when someone forced her into the alley and hit her on the head with a brick. Then, whoever it was, dragged her body to the alley behind the store."

"Oh, my lord," Lenora shuddered, covering her face with her hands. "How horrible."

"My sister and I went down to the crime scene when we were awakened by the police cars in the middle of the night," Beck said, adding, "We live above the bookstore."

Lenora looked up, her mascara slightly smudged as a tear slipped down her cheek. "You were there? Oh, how awful for you to have to witness that."

Beck's mind flashed back to seeing Peggy Davidson's body lying under the sheet, and she choked back a tear herself.

"At first they thought it was a mugging," Beck told her. "But now, they believe it may have been more personal because she was hit several times with the brick. It appeared that whoever killed her, wanted to be sure she was dead."

Lenora stared at her in shock, and the tears started to flow. "Oh no. Poor, poor, Peggy. Joe told me that she had been mugged. But this. Why? Why would someone do that to her? She was on vacation. A mugging I could understand. But why would someone want to murder Peggy?"

Beck shook her head. "That's what we've been trying to figure out. I don't know if you heard that her emerald ring was stolen?" The woman nodded as Beck continued. "But nothing else was taken. Her shoulder purse was still strapped to her with a few hundred dollars in it, and she had on an expensive necklace and watch, neither of which was taken."

Lenora frowned and glanced out the window toward the beach. She dabbed her eye with a tissue. "Her ring was extremely valuable. I remember when her husband gave it to her. She was so proud of it. We told her she should be careful and only wear it on special occasions, but she wouldn't hear of it. It symbolized her husband's love for her, and she wore it all the time. She had it on when they visited us the day before."

Lenora dabbed her eyes again and then folded the tissue in her lap. "I hope that ring didn't get her killed."

"Tell me about her visit," Beck prompted. "Did she seem concerned about anything? Was she having a problem with anyone?"

Lenora shook her head. "No, she seemed fine. She seemed very happy to be spending time with her son. They were so close."

"And her daughter-in-law, Lisa? Were they close, too?"

Lenora's eyebrows knitted together slightly. She seemed to grow a little uncomfortable.

"Well, I wouldn't say they were close, but they seemed to be adjusting." Beck could tell Lenora was the type of person who rarely spoke ill of anyone and didn't like to portray people in a bad light.

"Adjusting?" Beck asked.

"I don't want to be unkind," Lenora said gently. "But I don't believe Lisa would have been Peggy's first choice for Joe."

Beck raised an eyebrow. "Really? Why was that?"

"Well," she seemed to grow increasingly uncomfortable.

"I wouldn't ask in any other circumstance," Beck assured her. "I'm not a gossip. I'm just trying to learn as much as I can about your friend so we can figure out what happened to her."

Lenora stopped and stared out the window for several moments. "I wouldn't want anything I say to get back to Joe. I wouldn't want him to think I was talking about him behind his back."

"Oh, no. Of course not. You can be assured I won't say a word."

"All right then." She seemed to brace herself. "It wasn't really a secret that Peggy feared Lisa was marrying Joe for his money. She came from a different background—which didn't matter, of course," she was quick to add. "But it was more that she seemed to relish so much in what money could buy. The gifts he bought her while they were dating were astonishing."

"What did he buy her?"

"A Mercedes convertible, for one. Can you believe it? He was totally besotted with her. And then they married so quickly."

Beck couldn't remember ever getting more than a bouquet of flowers from anyone she'd ever dated—and that was on Valentine's Day. A Mercedes! The shock must have shown in her eyes because Lenora made eye contact and nodded her head. "So, you see what I mean."

"I'm stunned. Did his mother try to stop Joe from marrying her?"

"Oh, yes. But it fell on deaf ears. Then the next thing she knew, they were married. They had a destination wedding on a trip to Hawaii. It was all very last minute.

Peggy flew out just so she wouldn't miss her only child's wedding. But she was so disappointed."

"About the wedding or his choice of bride?"

Lenora tilted her head and gave Beck a pained look. "Both, I'm afraid."

"And since they've been married, how did Peggy and her daughter-in-law get along?"

"Well, Peggy didn't get to see as much of her son as she wanted. They immediately moved down south of Hatteras, almost two hours away. When Peggy did visit, her daughter-in-law wasn't particularly warm, but there was no real animosity between them as far as I know. I know Peggy was really looking forward to this trip."

"How were they when they visited you here?"

"They seemed to be getting on pretty well during their visit with us. I thought Peggy might be warming up to her. We had a full day of activities planned and everyone had a lovely time. We drove them around the island pointing out historic homes, shopping on Worth Avenue, having lunch at The Breakers. The full Palm Beach experience."

Sounds like a day anyone would enjoy, Beck thought. She found herself wishing she had a friend like Lenora Palmer.

"My grandmother and I had Joe and Lisa over for dinner the other night," Beck told her. "I don't know if Joe mentioned it."

"He did," Lenora said, brightening. "He told me he enjoyed it so much, and it helped him to open up about his mother. He said it was the first time he'd been able to do that since her death."

"It was our pleasure," Beck assured her. "We just wanted to do something for them after what they'd been through."

"That was so kind of you and your grandmother."

Beck nodded. "Lisa's brother also came along."

Lenora's face darkened a shade. "He did? I didn't realize he was down here in Florida, too."

Beck nodded. "He's moved to Ft. Lauderdale and is looking for a job somewhere in South Florida."

"Hmm. Where Lisa goes, he's never far behind."

"They're pretty close, I take it?"

"They seem to be," Lenora answered with a shrug. "Peggy didn't like him."

"Why not? If you don't mind me asking."

"No, of course not, dear. We're sharing information in confidence."

"Exactly," Beck nodded.

“Peggy just saw Eric as a ne’er-do-well who she was afraid would try to get money out of Joe. Joe is such a blindly amiable young man. He sees only the good in people.”

He must be a lot like Lenora, Beck thought. She could see how painful this conversation was for her. Beck had discovered at her ripe old age of twenty-nine that quite often the wealthiest people were also the kindest. Though, she conceded, that may well have been because they just didn’t have as much to worry about.

Chapter Twenty-Four

A thought occurred to Beck. "Well, if Eric is seriously looking for a job down here in South Florida, does that mean that Joe and Lisa are considering moving down here, too?"

Lenora's eyes lit up. "Oh, I would love it if they did. We don't have any children, and my godson is the closest we've ever come."

Beck tried not to let the surprise show on her face. This huge home they lived in was only for her and her husband.

Lenora continued, "I don't know if Joe told you, but my husband is developing the SeaBreeze Point resort up your way. When they were here the other day, Joe seemed extremely interested in investing in it. Maybe they'll end up moving there."

Beck had heard about the resort many times both from breakfast conversations among the townies, as well as from her grandmother's many complaints on the subject. No one was in favor of the massive project on heretofore untouched oceanfront land. Beck herself didn't care that much, nor did much of the town's younger population, who saw it as the inevitable result of progress. But for people who had lived in the area for years, the new development felt like an affront. For the first time today, Beck was glad Grammy hadn't accompanied her.

Beck avoided any controversy in her response. "I'm sure it would be wonderful for you if your godson was closer by," she said.

She wondered if Peggy Davidson had also considered moving to Florida and living in the development, and asked Lenora the question.

"Oh no," Lenora said adamantly. "Peggy was very much an Outer Banks person. She never would have left there. Her roots ran deep. In fact, my husband asked her if she was interested in investing in SeaBreeze Point, but she had absolutely no interest."

Mention of the Outer Banks turned Beck in a different direction. "Speaking of the Outer Banks, up in the Kitty Hawk area, I understand Peggy was really into volunteer work. Is there anyone up there I could talk to who was particularly close to Peggy?"

Lenora nodded immediately and picked up her cell phone from the coffee table. "You must speak to Janie Foster. She was Peggy's closest friend up there." She clicked through her phone numbers and then read off Janie Foster's number. Beck typed it into her phone. "If you find out anything from Peggy, you must let me know."

"Absolutely," Beck told her, pleased that Lenora was so open to her questions.

Beck would ask Janie Foster the same thing, but she asked Lenora, "Was there anybody up where she's from that she had any particular problems with? I guess a better way to phrase it is, did Peggy have any enemies?"

Lenora's forehead creased and she shook her head as she tried to think of anyone who hated Peggy Davidson enough to kill her.

"No one. She never mentioned having any problems with anyone that she ever told me about. She had very positive relationships with everyone because she was involved in so many volunteer activities."

Beck was just about to thank Lenora for her time and leave when she remembered one of the main questions she wanted to ask Peggy Davidson's closest friend since high school. What an idiot you are, she chastised herself. She couldn't believe she almost forgot.

"Lenora, I haven't mentioned to you who the author was at our book signing that Peggy attended. Marcia Graybill?"

Lenora didn't react to the name, so Beck continued. "She's a pretty famous mystery writer. Peggy said she went to your high school. Do you have any recollection of her?"

Lenora seemed surprised at the connection. "A famous author went to our high school? That's interesting. I don't recognize the name. I wonder what her maiden name was?"

Beck recalled that Peggy had mentioned a name, but she couldn't remember what it was.

"You wouldn't happen to have a high school yearbook, would you? Maybe we could figure out who she is."

Lenora seemed excited by the idea. "I would love to know who it is, and yes, I do have my old high school annual. Actually, I was just looking through it a couple of days ago. I pulled it out after I heard about Peggy. To reminisce, I guess." Her eyes began to mist again, and she quickly stood up. "Let me go get it. It's upstairs."

While Lenora was gone, Beck stood up and strolled down the long sunroom, admiring the potted crotons, the variety of colorful orchids, and the huge hanging baskets of air plants and ferns with stems so long they almost reached the ground. Stopping to admire the view of the beach, she saw a wild rabbit hop into the dunes that separated their large back yard from the beach. Glancing toward the other side of the lawn, she noticed a wide patio and swimming pool.

"Here we are," Lenora announced, holding up the book as she entered the room.

"I was just admiring your air plants," Beck said, as she walked down the room toward her hostess. "I think they're the prettiest ones I've ever seen."

"Well, thank you," Lenora said, obviously pleased. "My absolute favorite plant. And so easy to grow and take care of. Just spray them with water every week or so and they just thrive."

"The sun back here seems perfect for them," Beck told her. "They're really flourishing."

Beck sat back down on the couch next to Lenora, eyeing the light brown laminate cover of the yearbook that depicted a dark background shadow of a pair of antlers. The Deerwood High Bucks, the title read. If her math was correct, the yearbook was from forty seven-years before, which would have been their senior year.

Lenora thumbed through the book to the senior portrait section. It seemed to be a fairly large graduating class. Beck guessed there were at least two hundred photos.

“Here’s Peggy,” she said, pointing to the photo of a carefully posed, and totally unrecognizable to Beck, Peggy Pope. Her shoulder-length brown hair was teased in the front and curled into a flip as was the fashion of the day. A single string of pearls hung from her neck as the high school senior smiled demurely at the camera.

“She was so pretty,” Beck said.

“Oh yes,” Lenora agreed. “Peggy was very attractive. And popular.” She flipped a few pages forward in the yearbook until she found a half-page photo of a slender girl in a white tennis outfit swinging an old-fashioned wooden racket. “But this one is my favorite picture of her.”

Beck couldn't believe she was looking at the same person she'd met in her bookstore. The girl in this photo had to be more than one hundred pounds lighter than the woman who had come to the book signing.

Lenora noticed the surprised expression on Beck's face. "This is how I'll always remember Peggy," she said. "The years take their toll on all of us."

Beck nodded as Lenora flipped through the pages.

"And where is your picture?" Beck coaxed with a playful smile.

Lenora acted like she didn't want to show her but then thumbed quickly to the page.

"The years have taken their toll on me, too," the older woman replied with a laugh, an attractive set of crow's feet crinkling next to her eyes. From their pattern, it was easy to see that this pleasant woman had smiled a lot throughout her life.

Beck immediately recognized Lenora with her sparkling eyes and contagious smile standing on the top of a pyramid of cheerleaders in their short brown and yellow uniforms.

"Look at you!" Beck exclaimed, pointing to the picture. "I would recognize you anywhere."

Lenora's face lit up. "Oh, thank you. What fun we had! Those were the days."

Beck read the description under the picture. "So, you were the head cheerleader?"

Lenora nodded with a grin. "When I think of what my body was able to do back then! The jumps. The backflips. It makes me hurt just to think about it."

Beck laughed. People could say what they wanted about cheerleaders, but it looked as difficult as any sport she'd ever seen. She certainly knew she never could have done it. Being a nonathletic bookworm herself, and basically an introvert, becoming a cheerleader had never entered her mind.

"Now, let's see," Lenora said, flipping back to the portrait section. "What was the author's name again?"

"Marcia Graybill."

"I doubt we'll find her under that name, but let's check just to be sure." Lenora found the G's and moved her finely manicured forefinger down the page. "Grant, Gratton, Graves, Grazer. No Graybill. That must be her married name."

"Why don't we start at the beginning and just look for someone named Marcia," Beck suggested.

Lenora turned back the pages and carefully moved her finger row by row. There was a Marcia Brannon, but she looked nothing like the author. Two pages later, her finger stopped under the name Marcia Cox.

"May I?" Beck asked, pulling the yearbook toward her so she could take a closer look. The girl in the photo had long brown hair, parted in the middle, and heavy eye make-up. But there was something in those eyes and the shape of the nose. Beck felt sure she was staring at eighteen-year-old Marcia Graybill.

"This is her," Beck said, turning to look at Lenora. "Marcia Cox. Do you remember her?"

Lenora peered at the picture and then she gave Beck a peculiar look.

"She's a famous author now?" She sounded incredulous. "Marcia Cox?"

Beck nodded. It was obvious Lenora remembered her. "Marcia Graybill now."

"I must say, I'm shocked."

"Why?" Beck asked. "Wasn't she a good student?"

Lenora shrugged. "Well, I don't really know about that. I think I only had gym with her. But the Marcia Cox I remember had a lot of problems."

"She mentioned during her speech that she had a difficult childhood," Beck told her.

"I don't really know about her childhood or her home life, but in high school she was really into drugs. And she was arrested, more than once, both for drugs and for shoplifting. I think she even broke into some houses."

"Really?" It was hard for Beck to imagine the glamorous Marcia Graybill in jail for breaking and entering.

"In fact, I remember police cars coming to the school more than once to arrest her. They handcuffed her and took her away in the police car. It was the talk of the school. After her last arrest, she never came back. I don't know what happened to her after that. We all thought she might be locked up."

No wonder Marcia Graybill didn't want to talk about her high school days with Peggy Davidson. Not a lot of pleasant memories there.

"You remembered everything about her so quickly," Beck said. "I'm surprised Peggy didn't remember more about her, too. She knew she knew her, but couldn't remember any details."

Lenora gave her a sad look. "Peggy had been struggling the past couple of years with some memory issues. Honestly, I'm surprised she remembered her at all."

Beck was about to tell Lenora how successful Marcia had become as a writer when the front door slammed. Lenora jumped up and hurried toward the living room.

"Jordan's home. I'm so glad you'll get to meet him," she called over her shoulder as she rushed out of the sunroom.

A few moments later she reappeared with a distinguished-looking man in a grey suit carrying a briefcase. He had a full head of salt-and-pepper hair, wore wire-rimmed glasses, and appeared to be a few years younger than Lenora. Like her, he had aged extremely well.

Beck stood up to be introduced. Her husband was polite, but not particularly warm. He seemed unclear on who she was and why she was there.

"Dear, this is the woman who owns the bookstore in Manatee Beach where Peggy spent her last evening," Lenora told him. "She dropped by to give me her condolences. I didn't get a chance to tell you this morning that she would be stopping by."

The information seemed to make him a little uncomfortable. Beck realized some people just didn't like talking about death.

"A sad business," he said somberly. "Lenora has taken it very hard."

Lenora caught her husband up on the news about the murder. He listened intently, but didn't ask any questions or offer any theories.

"They'd just been here for a visit the day before. Who would have thought?" he said, shaking his head. "We were talking about my new development SeaBreeze Point. Being from Manatee Beach, you've probably heard about it?"

Beck nodded. "Yes, there's been a lot of coverage of it in the newspapers. How is it coming along?"

He pursed his lips. "Behind schedule, unfortunately. But we hope to have Phase One completed by the end of the year."

"Lenora said that Joe Davidson might be interested in investing there," Beck said. "It would be nice if they moved to town."

Jordan Palmer sent his wife a surprised look. "Well, yes. They're thinking about it. They like the area. We'll have to see what they decide."

"I would love it if they moved down here," Lenora said wistfully.

"I know you would, dear," Palmer said patting her knee and standing up. "If you'll excuse me," he said to Beck before leaving the room. "It was very nice meeting you."

Beck took that as her cue to leave and she stood up, too. "I'd better be going," she told Lenora. "I've taken enough of your time."

"Oh, not at all," Lenora said, rising to join her. "I've thoroughly enjoyed your visit. You've answered so many questions I've been wondering about. The worst thing is not knowing. You will keep in touch, I hope, with any further developments?"

"Of course, I will," Beck assured her. "And thank you for all the information about Peggy, too. I appreciate it more than you know."

They hugged goodbye at the door, and Beck felt as if she'd made a new friend. She hoped she'd see Lenora Palmer again.

When Beck pulled out of the long driveway onto the beach road, she didn't feel like heading back to Manatee Beach quite yet. She decided to treat herself to a shopping excursion before she left Palm Beach. Not to Worth

Avenue—Palm Beach's equivalent to Beverly Hills' Rodeo Drive—but rather to her favorite consignment shops where the rich and famous took their rarely worn garments to make room in their closets for newer ones.

She'd seen Oscar-worthy gowns that the mavens of Palm Beach society had worn to charity balls that sold for pennies on the dollar. A $10,000 designer gown worn once and then discarded might sell for three hundred dollars in a Palm Beach consignment shop. Of course, it wasn't a Versace or Valentino gown that Beck was seeking. She wouldn't have anywhere to wear it, anyway. No, she was just in search of a comfortable everyday blouse or skirt that she could wear to work in the bookstore. And she found one. A beautiful, long-sleeved, white eyelet blouse from St. John that still had the seven hundred dollar price tag on it! It was a size smaller than she normally wore, but she knew expensive clothes usually ran big. She tried it on and it fit fine. She happily paid the asking price of thirty-five dollars.

Before she left, she wanted to buy small gifts for Grammy and Lizzie. In the next consignment shop she went to down the street, she found a beautiful silver barrette that she thought would look lovely in her sister's hair. It was sterling silver, and she couldn't believe she was able to get it for the bargain price of six dollars. Her grandmother liked to wear broaches on her blouses or coat lapels, so when Beck found a hand-painted ceramic pin of an angelfish for four dollars, she snatched it up.

Driving home she felt a euphoria come over her. She wasn't sure if it came from her bargain purchases or from all the helpful information she'd gathered from Lenora Palmer. Probably both, she decided.

Chapter Twenty-Five

Beck arrived home from Palm Beach just as Beach Reads was closing. She was surprised to find Lizzie wiping down the tables and Teddy sweeping the floors.

"Well, this is unexpected!" Beck exclaimed.

She'd anticipated having those tasks waiting for her when she got home. "I hope Grammy didn't make you do this," she said to Lizzie.

"Not at all," Lizzie said, glancing up from the table with a grin. "I volunteered us. And I want to know what you found out!"

It felt so comforting to Beck to have family support for her investigative project.

"Quite a bit," Beck said, setting her shopping bag on the counter and sitting down on a stool.

Grammy finished drying a coffee cup and put down the dish towel. “I can’t wait to hear about it!”

Lizzie threw the kitchen rag she’d been using into a hamper and sat down on the stool next to Beck. Teddy kept sweeping and looked disinterested. Beck surmised he did pretty much anything Lizzie told him to do, as most of her boyfriends did.

First, though, Beck opened her shopping bag and told them about her shopping expedition. She pulled out the seven hundred dollar blouse and told them how much she’d paid for it.

“Are you kidding me?” Lizzie said in wonder. “Thirty-five dollars? I want to go shopping down there.”

“We will sometime, but for now I bought you this.” Beck reached into the bag and handed Lizzie the silver barrette. “It’s sterling silver.”

“Wow! It’s gorgeous,” Lizzie said, immediately clipping it into her hair. “How much was it?”

“Lizzie!” her grandmother scolded. “It’s impolite to ask how much a gift cost.”

“Yeah, but –” Lizzie began.

“And this is for you, Grammy,” Beck said, handing her grandmother the colorful angelfish pin. “I know how much you like broaches.”

Her grandmother's eyes lit up. She was obviously pleased. "It's beautiful! I know exactly the blouse I'll wear it with. Thank you, Beck."

"Yeah, thanks, Beck," Lizzie added.

"You're welcome. I'm just happy both of you like them."

"Love them!" Grammy said. She leaned forward putting both elbows on the counter and cupping her chin with her hands. "Now tell us what you found out."

Beck started off by describing the Palmer's huge oceanside house to her sister and grandmother, not leaving out a detail.

"Must be nice," her grandmother said. "It's a whole different world down there in Palm Beach than the way the rest of us live."

"But she was so nice, Grammy," Beck said. "She had so much class. I've never felt more welcomed in my life."

"Well, that is nice," Grammy gave her. "I guess people with that kind of money don't have a worry in the world."

Lizzie had a dazed look in her eye. "I wanna have a house on the beach like that someday," she mused. "That would be so cool."

"Well, you better get yourself back in college then," her grandmother chastised her. "You aren't going to have a house like that on a lifeguard's salary."

"Ugh," Lizzie groaned. "Forget I said anything. So, what did that rich lady say about 'the victim?'" Lizzie asked, using air quotes.

Beck leaned forward and lowered her voice. "Now we have to keep this just between us, right? Wouldn't want this information to get around town."

They both quickly nodded in agreement. The store had just closed so there were no customers. She glanced across the store at Teddy sweeping, but he had earphones on and seemed oblivious to them.

"Well, she said that Lisa, Peggy's daughter-in-law, was really all about Joe's money and that he actually bought her a Mercedes convertible while they were dating."

"That is sick!" Lizzie exclaimed. "Does he have any younger brothers?"

"Lizzie!"

"Just kidding," Lizzie replied with a giggle. She added, "That is pretty money-grubbing."

Grammy frowned. "I hate to hear that. Lisa seems like such a nice gal. And Joe is just salt of the earth."

"Joe is great," Beck agreed. "But it really made me wonder about Lisa. His mother was against the wedding. They got married after only six months, in a spur-of-the-moment destination wedding in Hawaii. Peggy flew out for it, but she wasn't happy about them getting married at all."

"Six months is fast," Grammy agreed. "I hope she's not a gold-digger. Or worse. A murderer. I like her."

Beck continued, "Peggy didn't like her brother Eric either, Lenora said."

"Oh?" Grammy asked. "What did she say about the brother?"

"Just that he's kind of a ne'er-do-well, and she's afraid he's after Joe's money, too."

"What's a naredwell?" Lizzie asked.

"It's ne're-do-well. Like never-do-well," Beck told her. "It's somebody who tries out lots of different jobs, but is never good at any of them and is usually unemployed."

Lizzie nodded. "Oh. Okay. Why don't they just say never-do-well? It would be a lot easier to understand."

"I don't know, Lizzie," Beck said impatiently. "It's old English or something. Can I please get back to my story?"

Lizzie shrugged and rolled her eyes. "Whatever! I was just asking."

Beck took a deep breath. Her sister could be so annoying sometimes, but she had to remember that Lizzie did something that day that she hadn't done in a long time. She came in and helped clean up the bookstore. "I'm sorry, Lizzie," Beck said apologetically. "I'm just tired. It's been a long day."

"It's okay," Lizzie replied. "Don't worry about it."

"Anyway," Beck said, drawing out the word, "Lenora felt that if Eric is looking to move down here, then Joe and Lisa probably are, too. And probably to SeaBreeze Point, because Joe really liked it there."

"SeaBreeze Point!" Grammy appeared on the verge of a monologue about the negatives of the controversial resort development.

Beck held up her hand. "I know how you feel about it, Grammy, but that's a discussion for another time. The point is, Joe is considering becoming an investor."

Grammy looked like she was about to bite her tongue off. She obviously had a lot to say on the subject. But Beck didn't want to get off on that tangent and continued.

"That was about all on the subject of Lisa, Joe, and Eric," Beck said. "Lenora said she didn't know anybody who was an enemy of Peggy Davidson, but she gave me the phone number of Peggy's best friend up in the Outer Banks. Janie something. I'm going to call her to see what I can find out."

Teddy approached them with a dustpan full of debris. "I'll go ahead and take the garbage out," he said, walking into the kitchen and dumping the dustpan into the garbage can. He leaned the broom against the wall and bagged up the garbage.

"Thank you, Teddy," Grammy told him. "That would be a big help."

After he closed the kitchen door, Beck said to Lizzie. "You've got a good one there, Lizzie. I hope you appreciate him."

Lizzie shrugged. "I mean, I do. I guess."

Grammy interjected, "What did you find out about the author? Anything? That's what I'm really interested in."

Beck's face lit up. "Yes! A lot. I'm going to call her next. And I want to talk to her husband, too."

"Oh good! I was hoping you'd find out about what the big secret was from her high school days," Grammy said.

“Well,” Beck began, “It turns out that in high school, Marcia Graybill, Marcia Cox then, was quite the druggie, and also was arrested for shoplifting and breaking and entering, too. Maybe to support her habit, I don’t know. The police came to the school a few times, handcuffed her, and took her to jail.”

Lizzie stared at her incredulously. “That blonde lady who was signing books the other night did that?”

Beck gave her sister a half-smile. She always seemed to forget that older people were young once, too. “It was the seventies, Lizzie. Teenagers have been getting into trouble for a long time.”

Grammy seemed as shocked as Lizzie. “I’m sure she wouldn’t want her readers to know that about her past.”

The back door opened and Teddy came back into the kitchen. He came around the counter and sat down next to Lizzie.

“I know,” Beck said. “But is it a reason to kill someone? And anyway, she was signing books the whole time and couldn’t have been out in the alley hitting Peggy Davidson with a brick.”

“But maybe her husband could,” Grammy suggested.

"Maybe. I'm definitely going to try to find out," Beck said.

Teddy elbowed Lizzie and whispered in her ear. "Teddy's hungry," Lizzie said, standing up. "We're gonna get some tacos."

"Okay," Beck told them. "Thanks so much for cleaning up for me! You two are the best!"

"No problem," Teddy answered with a dimpled smile.

Lizzie gave Beck a hug. "You're doing great, Sis. I'm proud of you for doing this. I just know you're going to find out who did it before the police do!"

"Aww, thanks, Lizzie. I don't think the police are looking into Peggy's background at all. They just seem to think Scratchoff McLean did it to steal her ring."

Teddy had begun to gently pull Lizzie by the hand toward the door. "The guy's weird, for sure," Lizzie said over her shoulder to Beck, "but he doesn't seem like a murderer type to me."

Beck agreed. "I don't think so either."

When Teddy opened the front door, Lizzie waved goodbye. "Teddy's really hungry," she said. "Gotta go! Taco time."

Chapter Twenty-Six

When Beck woke up the next morning, she wondered if the police department had any luck in tracking down Marcia Graybill and her husband. She doubted very seriously that the author would come back to Manatee Beach of her own volition. If Devon wanted to talk to her, in all likelihood, he'd have to drive down to the Keys to interview her. According to the author's schedule, today was her last day in Florida. Then she was slated to fly to Texas to continue her book tour there. Beck wondered if the police considered her important enough to the case to send an officer to interview her.

If it wasn't nearly a five-hour drive one-way from Manatee Beach to Key West, Beck would have considered driving down to talk to the author and her husband in person. But it was just too far, and she couldn't afford to be away from the store for that long. A telephone call would have to do. She had Marcia Graybill's personal cell phone number and decided to give it a try. She had nothing to lose. The author might ignore her call, but the two of them had connected, and Beck thought she might be willing to talk to her.

But how should she approach the author? The more she thought about it, she decided the best strategy would be to try to talk to Ms. Graybill's husband. Afterall, Marcia Graybill had been busy signing books at the time Peggy Davidson was supposedly killed. But it was possible, Beck supposed, that she could have directed her husband to do it. He did seem to be at her beck and call, even holding her purse as he waited around the entire evening for her to finish signing books.

Even if they weren't involved in her murder, the author's husband had what may have been Peggy's last conversation with her. Beck wanted to know what they talked about and if the conversation had anything to do with the author's less-than-stellar high school days.

After the last of their breakfast customers left the store, Beck asked her grandmother if she would make sure Beck wasn't disturbed while she called Marcia Graybill from the upstairs living room. Grammy readily agreed and stayed downstairs to take care of any late morning customers.

Sitting down in an armchair with her feet propped up on an ottoman, legal pad in her lap, Beck punched in Marcia Graybill's phone number. The phone rang four times before the author picked up with a curious "Hello?"

Beck sat up straighter in her chair. "Ms. Graybill? It's Beck from Manatee Beach."

"Beck?" There was a long pause. "Oh, Beck! How are you, dear? It's good to hear from you."

"How is your tour going?" Beck asked to break the ice.

"Oh, you know. Ups and downs. Miami was a nightmare. Not handled well at all."

"I'm sorry to hear that."

"Actually, Beck, I think your event was one of the best ones we've had. Definitely the best in Florida. Very well organized."

Beck's heart rate sped up. What a wonderful compliment. "Why thank you, Ms. Graybill. That means so much to me."

"You are most welcome. And I haven't forgotten our little talk. I've been spending more time with each of my fans, and I can't tell how much it means to them."

Beck was thrilled to hear that. “I’m just so glad I was able to say something that was helpful to you.”

“You certainly did, my dear. Now, is there something I can help you with, Beck?”

“Ms. Graybill, I have some unpleasant news,” Beck told her, although she believed the author was already aware. “The reason I’m calling is to tell you that the woman at your book signing here—the one who knew you from high school—was actually murdered when she was walking back to the hotel from the event. Maybe you remember, I called you that night when her son was looking for her.” Beck didn’t know if the author would remember the phone call or not, she was so drunk that night.

There was a pause, a long pause. “I did hear that,” the author replied finally. “The police called us in Miami and told us. It sounds like it was a mugging. For some reason, though, they wanted us to come back up there. But we don’t know anything about it, and I told them we couldn’t come back. My schedule is too tight.”

“I wasn’t sure if you knew or not,” Beck told her. “I thought you would want to know since you went to high school with Peggy.”

Another long pause. "Well, of course, I'm sorry the woman is dead, but we weren't close and, obviously, I don't know anything about her murder."

Beck sensed the author was about to end the conversation so she decided to try another route. "She was still carrying the autographed copy of your book when her body was found."

"Oh, my," the author gasped.

"She was a fan. It must have felt good to have someone you went to high school with so many years ago be one of your fans today."

The author's voice softened. "I hadn't really thought about it that way, but yes, I suppose it does. Especially since she and some of her friends weren't very kind to me back then."

"Oh no," Beck said, again asking a question she already knew the answer to. "Why not?"

The author sighed. "You heard me talk about my difficult childhood in poverty. Well, with my background, it wasn't easy attending a high school with so many privileged students. I wasn't able to afford the wardrobe, the lifestyle, to fit in. I tried. God knows I tried. But I made some major mistakes that alienated me even more, mistakes I'd like to forget."

"Did Peggy bring that up to you?"

"No, I'm not sure if she even remembered. Which was a blessing."

"I wonder, Ms. Graybill, if you would mind if I spoke to your husband? I noticed him talking to Peggy while you were signing books. I think he may have been the last person to talk to her. Perhaps she said something to him that might shed light on what happened to her?"

The author didn't immediately respond, so Beck continued. "I've felt so guilty about what happened to her. I can't get past the feeling that if I hadn't encouraged her to come to the book signing, she might still be alive."

"Now, dear," the author responded immediately, "you can't blame yourself. We all have free will, and she did what she wanted to do. How could you know she would be mugged on her way home?"

"Thank you, Ms. Graybill. I appreciate your saying that. It's just hard. Do you think I could speak to your husband for a couple of minutes? It might help."

"Certainly, dear. He's right here."

Beck heard the muffled voices as the author spoke to her husband. He sounded like he didn't want to talk to her. But Ms. Graybill apparently convinced him because a moment later a deep male voice came on the phone. “Hello?”

“Mr. Graybill. I’m sorry to bother you—” Beck began.

“My name is not Graybill. That’s my wife’s name. My name is Robert Wells.”

Great start, Beck thought, angry with herself. She should have doublechecked his name before she called.

“I’m so sorry, Mr. Wells,” Beck apologized. She took a calming breath. “Thank you so much for talking to me. As I told your wife, I have been feeling so guilty and partially responsible for Peggy Davidson’s death because I encouraged her to come to the book signing that night.”

“Nonsense,” the man answered in a less than friendly tone. “It’s not your fault someone left your place of business and got mugged.”

Beck ignored the comment and asked the author’s husband the question she really wanted to know.

“I noticed you and the woman who was killed talking while you were waiting for your wife to finish signing books. I was wondering if you could remember what you talked about, and if perhaps she said anything that might point to who killed her.”

"I understood she was mugged," he answered in a clipped voice.

"Well, actually, the police have determined that it probably wasn't a mugging, that she was killed by someone who specifically wanted her dead."

"Hmm. Well, be that as it may, I don't have a clue what I talked about to some fan of Marcia's at a book signing several days ago."

Beck wasn't going to give up. This interview was too important to her. And she knew she only had one shot.

"Could you try to think back, Mr. Wells," Beck implored. "It's really important."

An exasperated sigh came over the phone. It annoyed Beck, but she knew she had to tread easily.

"A woman died, Mr. Wells. You were probably the last person who spoke to her. Could you try?"

Another sigh, and then, "Well, let me think back and see if I can remember anything."

Beck tried to jolt his memory. "The woman who was killed, Peggy Davidson, went to high school with your wife. She may have talked to you about that."

That seemed to do the trick. "Ah, I do remember that. A heavyset woman who looked much older than my wife?"

Beck's heart leapt that at least he remembered something, though she wasn't thrilled to hear the unflattering description of the dead woman. "Yes, that was her. Did she say anything about going to high school with your wife?"

"Yes, I do remember her saying something about them going to school together in North Carolina. But that's all I recall. She didn't seem to remember if they had classes together, or if they were friends. Her memory seemed a bit scattered."

"Did she say anything else? I noticed you talked for several minutes."

"Yes, I remember I couldn't get away from her. She babbled on about being from the Outer Banks of North Carolina, I believe, and that she was on vacation. But that's about all I remember. I really wasn't listening that closely."

"Nothing else," Beck asked, disappointed.

"No, I don't think—" He paused, thoughtfully and then added, "You know, I do remember her saying something odd. She got a strange look on her face and muttered something like 'she died' or 'he died.' I remember thinking, 'Who died?' Then she said she had to tell her son something, and she rushed out of the store."

That was strange. Beck hadn't heard anything like that mentioned before.

"What happened right before that? Was she looking at someone in particular, or maybe out the window?"

"I didn't notice anything in particular. I kept looking over at my wife. I wasn't really looking at the woman."

Beck tried to think quickly. She knew she was going out on a limb with this question, but she wanted to know.

"Were you aware of your wife's difficult high school experiences?"

"What does that have to do with anything?" He sounded irritated. "But yes, I was aware she didn't have an easy time of it. I figured bumping into an old high school acquaintance that night wouldn't exactly make her day and that I would hear about it afterward. Which I did."

"Your wife was upset?"

He didn't reply for several moments and when he did, he was annoyed. "That's really none of your business, is it? You're getting awfully nosy. Who do you think you are, some Annabelle James wannabe?" He was alluding to the name of the amateur sleuth in his wife's cozy mysteries.

"I'm sorry," Beck said apologetically. "I'm just trying to make sense of this."

"If that'll be all," he replied brusquely.

"Just, is there anything else you can think of from that night? Did you happen to go outside the store and maybe notice anything?"

"Go outside the store? No. I just spent another evening in a bookstore in a strange city waiting for my wife. That has become the story of my life."

Whoa, Beck thought. Sounds a little bitter. But she was pleased with the new information she'd gotten.

"Thank you so much, Mr. Wells. I appreciate your talking to me. Would you please thank your wife, too? I hope the rest of your tour goes well."

"Thank you. Goodbye." The phone clicked off before she had a chance to respond.

Holding the phone away from her ear, Beck felt disappointed the conversation had taken a downturn at the end. But at least she'd learned some valuable information, and she couldn't wait to tell her grandmother what she'd found out.

But what did it mean?

Chapter Twenty-Seven

Grammy couldn't figure out either what Peggy Davidson had meant by the comment "She died" or "He died." And then running off to tell her son. Had Robert Wells heard her right? Did it have something to do with his wife's high school days? Who died? They both threw out a lot of possible theories, but none really made much sense.

Two lunch customers came into the store so they had to cut their discussion short. The tourists both ordered a sandwich and a scone. Grammy fixed the sandwiches, and Beck plated the scones, the last two they had. A bigger-than-usual breakfast crowd had wiped out most of their pastries. Scones were, by far, the most popular order on their limited menu. Several locals had a morning ritual of stopping by the bookstore to have a cup of coffee and a scone and read the morning paper. Newspaper sales had become a large part of their business, and they carried several, including *The Miami Herald* and *The New York Times*.

"Beck, would you mind running down to the bakery and getting some more scones?" her grandmother asked. "It's too early in the day for us to run out."

Beck was delighted to have a chance to get out of the store for a little while in the middle of the day. "Sure. I'd love to, Grammy. I'll take Coquina with me."

The dog lay in her usual place in the corner of the kitchen, so Beck called to her over the counter. "Coquina. C'mon girl. Let's go for a walk." The large dog got awkwardly to her feet, walked sleepily to Beck, and stood perfectly still while Beck fastened her collar. "I'll be back soon, Grammy."

Her grandmother glanced up from the bowl of chicken salad she was mixing. "No rush. Coquina needs the exercise. I'll hold down the fort."

The weather outside was beautiful. A slight breeze came in off the ocean and the temperature topped off in the high seventies. A perfect spring day in Florida. Coquina took her time sniffing around the front porch of Beach Reads as Beck waited patiently. She tried to avoid making eye contact with Phil Merritt, who was sweeping the sidewalk in front of his jewelry store next door. She noticed him bend down to pick up the discards of a raw sugar packet that a customer from Beach Reads had apparently dropped. Lydia always complained about litter from the bookstore ending up on their sidewalk, and she felt sure Phil would report it to her.

"Hello, there," Phil called out. Beck looked up as if she were seeing him for the first time. "Oh, hi Phil. How's business?"

"Not too bad," he replied. He stopped sweeping and leaned the broom against the wall. Phil wore a crisp white shirt, tailored pants, and polished black shoes, his usual impeccable, at-work uniform. Putting his hands on his hips, he glanced around the street. "I think we're still getting some rubberneckers who want to hear about the murder."

Beck scrunched her nose. "How ghoulish," she muttered under her breath. Aloud she said, "I see the police tape is still up."

Phil pursed his lips. "I wish they'd get out here and take it down. They told us we can't use the back door as long as it's up. Most inconvenient."

"Have you heard any more from the police?" Beck asked.

"They—" Before he could answer, she heard the unmistakable shrill voice of Scratchoff McLean as he rolled up from behind her on his beach bike. His blond hair was a tangled mess, his tank top torn and dirty, and one of his well-worn flipflops fell off when he skidded to a stop. He backed up the bike and inched his toes through the dirt into the shoe.

"Well, hello there big fella." Scratchoff reached out his hand to pet Coquina who had leaped away from the bike and was leaning her huge body into Beck's leg.

"Coquina is a girl," Beck corrected.

"My mistake," Scratchoff apologized, continuing to pet the dog. "No offense meant, big girl."

Phil's face contorted into a frown at the interruption. He focused a critical stare at Scratchoff's appearance.

Beck turned back to Phil. "You were saying, Phil. About the police?"

He appeared not to want to answer in front of Scratchoff, but then he went ahead anyway.

"The police have continued to badger us. Just because the body was found behind our store, and she was missing a valuable piece of jewelry. You'd think they could be more discerning."

Scratchoff squinted at Phil. "That right? Well, I gotta say, I'm not too sad to hear that them po-lice are lookin' at somebody else besides just me for a change. We got po-lice cars drivin' past the motel at all hours of the day and night."

Phil scowled at him and crossed his arms. He obviously felt deeply offended to be viewed in the same category as Scratchoff in anything.

Beck told them, "I think the police are spending too much time focusing on that ring and not enough on Peggy Davidson's background. Whoever hit her all those times with that brick wanted her dead. They didn't need to do that to steal the ring."

"That's right smart, Miss Beck," Scratchoff complimented. "I think you're on to something there."

"I've been trying to figure some things out," Beck continued. "She was murdered after being in our bookstore. I feel a little responsible."

"Doing a little amateur detective work, eh?" Phil asked, with a chuckle. "Like the woman in that author's book who owned the—what was it called? The Dead & Breakfast Inn?"

"Yes, I guess you could say that—" Beck started to respond when Scratchoff gave a noisy greeting to someone who had walked up behind them. When Beck turned around, she was shocked to see Lisa Davidson's brother, Eric, standing right behind her. She felt immediately uncomfortable and wondered how long he'd been standing there listening. And what he'd heard.

Scratchoff, who since his lottery win had appointed himself the town's official greeter with tourists, introduced himself to Eric and started to introduce Beck.

"We've met," Beck interrupted. "Hello, Eric. Nice to see you again."

Eric nodded but didn't smile. He stopped to pet the dog.

"How much longer are you in town for?" Beck asked him.

"I'm leaving tomorrow," he said.

"Any luck job hunting?"

He shook his head. "Not really."

"Lookin' for work, are ya?" Scratchoff asked.

Eric nodded and clearly didn't want to engage in a conversation on the subject.

"I'd better get back," he said, ending the conversation and crossing the street.

"Don't believe I've seen that feller around before," Scratchoff said curiously.

Eric was far enough down the street that he couldn't hear their conversation. "He's Lisa Davidson's brother," Beck told them. "The daughter-in-law of the woman who was killed."

Phil glanced down the street after him. "We met his sister. She bought a bracelet from us the other day. Very nice young woman."

Beck nodded. She remembered Lydia telling them about it.

"Well, I'd better be getting along," Beck told them, tugging on Coquina's leash. "Grammy ran out of scones. I need to get to the bakery."

"You can't be havin' that," Scratchoff said with a big grin, pushing off on his bike. He called back over his shoulder as he pedaled, "And you know who to call if you ever have any leftover scones that you need to get rid of."

Phil raised his eyes to the heavens. "How did we ever get so unlucky to have to deal with that man on a daily basis?"

Beck laughed. "Oh, Scratchoff's not so bad. Every town has its characters."

Phil just shook his head and went back inside the store. When Beck passed the jewelry store, she saw Lydia staring curiously at her from behind the jewelry counter. There was no doubt in Beck's mind that Phil would be grilled about every word of their conversation.

Chapter Twenty-Eight

Beck had planned to call Peggy Davidson's friend Janie Foster in the Outer Banks that afternoon, but the bookstore got so busy she couldn't break away. A senior citizen center from up the coast brought a busload of residents to town for the afternoon, and the bookstore seemed to have been designated as their central meeting place. Not that she was complaining. Bus tours were fantastic for business, but they really kept Beck and Grammy hopping. Beck and her grandmother had been talking about hiring someone to help out, and another afternoon like this one would definitely seal the deal.

Thank goodness she'd bought two dozen more scones at the bakery because they almost sold out again. They did sell out of muffins, Danish, and sandwiches. And the store had a bigger day in book sales than they'd had in a couple of weeks, with the exception of the night of Marcia Graybill's book signing.

Lizzie stayed home for a rare evening and, since she'd gotten her paycheck that day, offered to treat them to a vegetarian pizza from Al's pizzeria two blocks down Ocean Avenue. Grammy and Beck were quick to accept the offer. The last thing either of them had the energy to do after their busy day was to cook dinner. The three O'Rourke women had a fun evening playing dominoes afterward. Grammy won, of course. She always did. But they hadn't had a family night like this since the Christmas holidays and it felt good.

Beck was dead tired, but she knew she couldn't go to bed until she took Coquina for her nightly walk. Lizzie volunteered, but she was already dressed for bed, so Beck told her she would do it. It was nearly eleven, and the restaurant across the street that was ablaze with light earlier in the evening was already closed. Clouds blanketed the sky, blocking out the moon and stars, and the only light on the street came from a dim streetlamp.

Beck walked Coquina late every night and never felt nervous about being out after dark. But since the murder, walking outside at night on the street, this street where the murder had taken place, felt uncomfortable. Eerie, really, especially on a cloudy night like tonight. She wished the Great Dane would hurry up, but Coquina was taking her sweet time, sniffing every stone. A strong, chilly breeze blew in off the Atlantic, and the palm trees along Ocean Avenue rustled wildly in the wind. Beck was tuned into every sound, listening to each wave crash in the distance, as she peered cautiously around. Normally, she would have walked Coquina farther down the street, but tonight she didn't want to veer too far from the front steps of the store.

After several minutes, Beck finally managed to coax the dog onto the porch. A glimmer of light came through the bookstore window, and when she glanced down, she noticed a discarded empty sugar packet on the sidewalk. Better to pick it up before it blows next door, she thought, bending over.

The loud crack of a car backfiring or a gunshot blasted, and she felt something whizz past her head and crash into the front door of the bookstore. Coquina yelped and started to bark frantically. Beck hit the ground and lay flat with her head buried in her arms, shaking. Had someone just shot at her?

Lying facedown on the sidewalk, her heart racing, Beck heard footsteps running away next to the restaurant across the street. A moment later, Lizzie was screaming her name from inside the store. Then the front door flew open and Lizzie was at her side, kneeling beside her.

"Beck! Are you okay? I heard a gunshot."

"Get down," Beck warned. "I think someone just shot at me."

Lizzie ducked down next to Beck. "Are you hurt?"

"I'm okay," she told Lizzie breathlessly. "I wasn't hit. I think I heard him run away."

Beck glanced up at the front door and saw the bullet hole. It just missed the glass pane. They both inched their way to the door, pushed it open, and then crawled inside.

Grammy reached the front door and waved them both inside. "Get inside quick. Whoever's out there, may try again." She slammed the door behind them.

Beck felt dizzy, and it took her a minute to stand up. Lizzie grabbed hold of her under her arms and helped her to stand. Coquina was still outside whining and lying on the sidewalk by the door. Beck panicked and thought maybe the dog had been hit. But when Lizzie opened the front door, the Great Dane crawled to her feet and ran into the building. Lizzie quickly went from window to window pulling down the blinds.

Beck sat down at one of the tables and leaned forward, placing her head between her knees. Coquina came over to her and licked her cheek, seeming to want to comfort her.

Grammy was already on the phone calling 911.

"Someone tried to kill you, Beck," Lizzie cried, hugging her sister. "Who would do something like that?"

"Maybe it was just a stray bullet?" Beck suggested, not wanting to believe the alternative, that someone out there actually wanted her dead.

Lizzie looked skeptical. "I hate to say it, but maybe someone is afraid you're getting too close."

"But I haven't found out that much," Beck countered.

"They may not know that, though," Grammy replied, agreeing with Lizzie's assessment. "Maybe you're turning over some stones that someone doesn't want turned over."

A few minutes later they heard police sirens, and before they knew it, police were swarming the building. Three squad cars had pulled up outside and officers with flashlights had fanned out down the street.

Devon was the last to arrive. Dressed in a pair of tight blue jeans and a yellow sports shirt, it was obvious he was off-duty and had been called in from home. His hair was wet and slicked back, like he'd just gotten out of the shower.

He immediately crossed the room to the table where Beck sat with her grandmother and sister and squatted down beside her.

"What happened?" he asked, his voice thick with concern. "I was told someone took a shot at you."

Beck nodded, and for the first time, her eyes misted at the realization of how close she had come to death. She fought back tears. She didn't want Devon to know how vulnerable she felt.

"I was on the front porch, coming back from walking Coquina—" she began. Her voice caught in her throat and she couldn't speak.

Lizzie finished her thought. "Somebody shot at her. The bullet hit the door. Thank God it missed her."

Devon reached out and touched Beck's arm. Something akin to an electric shock shot ran through her body. She lifted her tear-stained eyes to look at him.

"I thought it might be a car backfiring," she said. "But then I felt something fly past my ear, and I realized it was a bullet."

"Did you see anyone?" Devon asked.

Beck shook her head. "It was so dark. Everything was closed and there were no lights on and no moon. I couldn't see anything. I leaned down to pick up a piece of litter on the sidewalk. I guess that's what saved me. Afterward, I heard footsteps running away across the street."

Devon rubbed her arm. The simple movement seemed to awaken every nerve in her body.

"Beck, I don't understand," he said. "Why would someone want to shoot you? It doesn't make sense."

Grammy had been sitting silently by, but she finally spoke up.

"I think we all know why," she told Devon. "Beck's been doing some investigating into the murder of Peggy Davidson. And she's obviously made someone uncomfortable."

Devon's eyebrows knitted together into a frown. "Looking into the murder of Peggy Davidson? What do you mean?"

Lizzie glanced at her grandmother and then at Beck. She wasn't about to say anything.

Grammy, realizing she'd probably said too much, went mute, too. So, it was left up to Beck to respond.

Beck couldn't meet Devon's eyes. "I felt responsible, partly responsible anyway, for Peggy Davidson's death," she said, sneaking a peek at Devon's face. "I encouraged her to come to the book signing and then she was murdered on her way home. I was just asking some questions to see if I could help to figure out who did it."

Devon pulled his hand away from her arm and said to her, "Beck, look at me."

She lifted her gaze and met his eyes. "Leave the detective work to the police department. We'll find Peggy Davidson's killer. I know you mean well, but amateurs shouldn't get involved in murder investigations."

Beck felt her hackles rise again. Maybe Devon thought she was an amateur, but she knew she was more than that. She knew her instincts were as good as any homicide detective's.

When she didn't respond, he said to her, "Beck, promise me you'll stop snooping around into this murder. The police department has it well in hand."

She looked away and didn't answer him. Grammy and Lizzie saw the look on her face and knew she'd dug her heels in.

"Beck?" Devon said again. "This is serious. Someone took a shot at you. You've obviously hit a nerve with somebody. Do you want to tell me what you've been up to?"

Beck shook her head. "I'm sure it's nothing you'd be interested in. If I ever get any definitive information, I promise you'll be the first to know."

"Beck?" he said again. She looked away. He glanced at her sister and grandmother, both of whom gave him a noncommittal shrug.

"Beck," Devon said sternly. "I need to know. Do you have any idea who shot at you?"

Beck stared at the wall and shook her head. She wished she did have an idea of who had tried to kill her, but she didn't. "I'd tell you if I did."

Devon stood up, crossed his arms, and looked down at her. He sighed. "Beck, I don't want anything to happen to you. I get that you feel attached to this case, but please, let the police do our job. Don't get involved. It's too dangerous. There's a murderer on the loose."

Beck continued to look away, not making eye contact.

"Beck?" Devon said again.

She shrugged and didn't respond.

"I'm going to put a police detail on your store, so don't be surprised if you see police cruisers driving by every fifteen minutes or so. In the meantime, I'm going to ask you, beg you, for your own safety, to let go of any personal investigating that you may be involved in."

She still wouldn't look up at him.

He put his forefinger under her chin and tilted her face up toward his. "Will you please promise me that? I don't want anything to happen to you."

Beck looked into his deep brown eyes and was lost for a moment. But then she shifted her gaze and looked away. She wasn't making that promise to anyone.

Chapter Twenty-Nine

Grammy insisted that Beck take off the next day to recover from the trauma of the late-night attack. Lizzie took a leave day from her lifeguard job to stay home and help Grammy out in the store. Beck insisted that she was fine to work, but neither her sister nor her grandmother would hear of it.

Beck had a fitful night's sleep, including a nightmare of her near-miss with a bullet, so it felt good to sleep late the next morning. Lizzie pampered her by bringing a plate of muffins and scones and a teapot of Earl Grey tea to her in bed. She told Beck the police had stopped by earlier to be sure everyone was okay, and a patrol car had been driving by every few minutes since then. Devon had also called to check on her, and Grammy had spoken to him.

Grammy appeared at her door a few minutes later with a copy of the *New York Times* and the latest *Time* magazine. "I thought you might like to catch up on what's happening in the world," she said cheerfully, as she set the periodicals on the nightstand next to Beck's bed.

Beck plumped the pillow behind her and pulled herself up straighter. "Thanks, Grammy. I'll look at them. But what I was thinking of doing in a little while is calling Peggy Davidson's friend Janie Foster in North Carolina. I've really been wanting to talk to her."

Grammy put her hands on her hips and stared down at her granddaughter. "Now, Beck. I don't know if that's a good idea."

"Don't try to stop me, Grammy. Last night was just a minor setback."

"A minor setback?" Her grandmother was astounded. "You could have been killed. You told me this investigation of yours wouldn't be dangerous."

"This just tells me I'm getting close. I can't stop now, Grammy."

Grammy stood firm with her hands on her hips giving her granddaughter a hard stare. "I promised Devon on the phone this morning that I wouldn't let you do anything dangerous."

Devon! He needed to mind his own police business.

"Grammy, you're not being a good Watson. You're supposed to encourage me, not stop me from doing what I need to do."

"It's too dangerous, Beck. I don't want to lose my granddaughter."

Beck crossed her arms in front of her. This was going to be an O'Rourke standoff and Beck had no intention of losing it.

"It's just a phone call, Grammy. No one has to know. And who's a woman up in North Carolina going to tell, anyway?"

Her grandmother didn't answer, and Beck could tell that she had backed down a bit. "This means a lot to me, Grammy. I've come this far—I don't want to stop now."

Her grandmother sighed and pursed her lips. "Okay, I'll leave you alone for your phone call, and tell Lizzie not to come up. But please, Beck, let this be the end of it."

Beck wasn't making any promises. She told her grandmother, "Thank you," and asked her to close the bedroom door behind her.

For several moments, Beck considered how she should approach Janie Foster. Then, she reached for the legal pad and phone and scrolled through her phone numbers. She quickly found the number for Janie Foster that she had typed in when she was in Palm Beach. The phone rang three times before a female voice picked up.

"I'm trying to reach Janie Foster, the friend of Peggy Davidson," Beck said, trying to avert a hang-up in case the woman thought it was a sales call.

"This is Janie Foster," the woman answered in a surprised voice.

"Ms. Foster, my name is Beck O'Rourke. I own the bookstore in Manatee Beach, Florida, where your friend Peggy spent her last evening. She was killed right after she left our bookstore. As you might imagine, I've been quite distressed since her murder, and wondered if you might have a few minutes to talk to me?"

"Well," the woman sounded uncertain. "Yes, all right, I'll be happy to talk to you. But I don't know anything about it. Her son Joe called to tell me last week, and there was an article in the newspaper up here about the mugging. I've been absolutely devastated."

"I'm so sorry for your loss," Beck began. "I spoke to Lenora Palmer and she told me how close the two of you were."

"Oh, Lenora. Peggy's friend from high school. You talked to Lenora?"

"Yes, I drove down to Palm Beach to talk to her. The police seem to think Peggy's death had something to do with her emerald ring that was stolen, but I think there may have been more to it."

"Why do you think that?"

Beck hesitated. She didn't want to upset the woman with too much gory detail about how her friend had been killed.

"Well, the extent of her injuries were more than what would be expected in a typical robbery. It appeared the murderer wanted to be sure Peggy was dead."

Peggy's friend choked up. "Oh, no. Poor, poor Peggy. She had been looking forward to the trip for so long, and then for this to happen."

"Looking forward to spending time with her son and daughter-in-law?" Beck asked.

"Yes," she answered, sniffling. "Peggy barely got to see them anymore since they married."

"If you don't mind me asking, how did Peggy get along with her new daughter-in-law?" Beck asked.

Janie Foster hesitated. "I wouldn't want Joe or his wife to know what I say."

"I won't say anything to them," Beck assured her. "You have my word, Ms. Foster."

"Oh, please call me Janie," the woman said.

"And call me Beck," she returned.

Janie paused before she spoke. "Well, Peggy didn't like Lisa one bit. She thought she was a gold-digger. And Peggy wasn't one to hold her tongue. I know that caused problems with Joe, too. They used to be so close, but since the wedding, they didn't talk nearly as much."

That was news to Beck. Joe seemed so broken up about his mother's death. Anyone would have thought they were as close as a mother and her adult son could be. But maybe he had feelings of guilt after her death for not spending as much time with her recently.

"I'm surprised they decided to take a vacation together," Beck said.

"That trip was more about real estate investments than it was about a vacation. Joe wanted his mother to invest in a big resort community down there, but Peggy didn't want to. Actually, it was Lenora Palmer's husband's development."

Beck's brain went into motion. Joe brought his mother down to Florida to get her to invest in a real estate venture that she wasn't interested in. Now that she was dead and Joe inherited everything, he was free to invest. But with all their money, was that a reason to kill someone? It didn't make sense. She couldn't see anyone doing that, let alone Joe. He seemed to be so much on the up-and-up, such a classy guy all the way around.

"Did Peggy feel pressured to invest?" Beck asked.

"I think she did," Janie Foster said. "She said the few times she had spoken to Joe since their marriage, the investment always came up in the conversation. I think half the reason she agreed to go to Florida to check the place out was so that she could spend some time with Joe. But she was absolutely against investing in it. She and her husband lost a lot of money in real estate during the recession and she wanted nothing to do with it."

Beck wondered just how much Lenora Palmer's husband needed Peggy's money for SeaBreeze Point. So many real estate investors took a bath during the recession. She figured he probably did, too. With Peggy out of the way, Palmer could more easily convince Joe to invest.

"Janie, did Peggy have any enemies that you know of? Anyone who might not be sad that she is gone?"

She seemed surprised by the question. "Enemies? Peggy didn't have any enemies. She led a very blessed life and made so many friends through all of her volunteer work. But in the past few years, she'd had so much loss. Her life wasn't as carefree as it was when her husband was alive."

"What kind of loss?"

"Well, of course, her husband dying unexpectedly of a heart attack a few years ago turned her world upside down. She was just starting to get over that when her only sister passed away. Then one of our best friends and her husband died in a fire. And two days before she left on the trip, her next-door neighbor fell off a ladder and broke his neck. She was upset that she wasn't able to go to his funeral."

So much death, Beck thought. She wondered if Peggy's last comment of "she died" or "he died" had anything to do with any of them.

"And then, of course," Janie continued, "her only child marries a woman he barely knows who she doesn't like. And then they move two hours away and she hardly ever sees him anymore. It was all very tough on her."

Beck continued to jot down notes as Janie Foster answered her questions. She found herself feeling very sorry for Peggy Davidson. It sounded as if her life had really spiraled downward after her husband's death.

"What did you think of Lisa? Do you think she's a gold-digger?"

The woman at the other end of the phone hesitated. "It's not for me to say. I don't know her well at all. All I know is that Peggy thought so. But to be fair, Peggy never thought anyone was good enough for her son."

"Did Peggy ever say anything about Lisa's brother, Eric?"

Janie answered immediately.

"Oh, she didn't like him at all. I think she was actually a little afraid of him. She worried that he might try to con Joe out of money."

"What made her think that?" Beck asked.

"Just his manner, I think. She did wonder if he had a criminal record. His personality seemed a little threatening to her. Apparently, he was pretty protective of his sister, so maybe that was why."

Beck heard someone in the background say something to her.

"I don't want to be rude," Janie said, "but my husband has a doctor's appointment that he needs to get to, and I'm driving him. If there's nothing else—"

"No, no," Beck said, grateful to have gotten the information she did. "Thank you. You've answered all of my questions. You've been very helpful, and I'm sorry to have kept you."

"I hope I've been able to be of some help. If you find you have more questions, feel free to call," she said. "Peggy was my best friend and I'll miss her dearly. So, I'm happy to help in any way I can."

Beck thanked her again and said goodbye.

Chapter Thirty

After she hung up, Beck took a few minutes to finish making notes of everything she'd learned from Janie Foster. She was beginning to feel that she had a very good picture of what Peggy Davidson's life was like before she came to Manatee Beach. There were definitely some points Beck wanted to follow up on with some online research, but she would do that later.

Now, she was anxious to get out of bed and begin the day. It was nearly one o'clock in the afternoon, and Beck couldn't remember the last time she'd stayed in bed so late. She showered, washed her hair and blew it dry, and then got dressed. When she descended the stairs to the bookstore, Lizzie was waiting on a table of late lunch customers, and her grandmother was checking out a customer buying a book at the cash register.

Beck strode directly to the front door, opened it, and checked out the bullet hole. It had missed the glass panes in the door and lodged in the door frame. The hole was at head level, and about the size of a dime, with splintered wood branching out from it in all directions. There were claw marks too, which she guessed came from the police digging the bullet out.

Looking at the bullet hole, Beck realized with dismay that if she hadn't bent down to pick up that piece of paper, the bullet could very well be lodged in her brain. The thought made her shudder, and she subconsciously took a step backward into the bookstore, stopping to peer around outside in all directions.

Lizzie was at her side within seconds. "What are you doing, Beck? Get back inside."

"I can't hide inside the rest of my life," she told her sister. "The person who shot at me is long gone. And I'm sure he wouldn't try anything in broad daylight."

"Maybe that's true," Lizzie said forcefully, "but it's best if you stay inside today. You need to rest. You've had a traumatic experience."

Beck knew her little sister was giving her good advice, advice she'd probably learned in her lifesaving training. She decided to listen to Lizzie and nodded her assent.

"Are we going to have to get a new door?" Beck asked, as her sister pushed the door shut. "That will be expensive."

"I was thinking about that," Lizzie answered. "I think we should leave it. Shows we can handle anything."

Beck's eyes brightened. She loved her sister's attitude. "I think I like that idea."

"That's my sister." Lizzie hugged her. "O'Rourke tough!"

Grammy stood next to the snack counter talking on her cell phone. When Beck and Lizzie approached, she reached out her hand with the phone to Beck. "It's your mother."

"Oh God," Beck muttered under her breath. "Here we go again."

Beck took hold of the phone, walked to the end of the counter, and sat down on a barstool. She summoned her most cheerful voice.

"Hi, Mom. How's everything in Montreal?"

"That doesn't matter," her mother began in her usual frank tone. "How are you? What in the world happened last night?"

"I'm fine, mom. Really," she began, and then gave her concerned mother a rundown of everything that had happened the night before.

"Beck, whatever you're doing, you need to stop. It's not worth risking your life."

Beck didn't respond. She didn't like to lie, so she wasn't going to tell her mother what she wanted to hear.

Beck heard a long sigh. "Look, honey, I know detective work is something you've always wanted to do. I understand that, probably more than you realize. I think you got that from me. But it's become too dangerous. Please tell me you'll stop."

"But I'm getting close, Mom. That's obvious. The killer is afraid I'm starting to figure it out."

Her mother didn't say anything for a long moment. "I know you have the brains to solve it, Beck. I have no doubt of that. But can't you just give what you've found out to the police and let them take it from here? I don't want anything to happen to you."

"The police are going in another direction, Mom. I don't think they'd listen to me anyway."

"Look, Beck. I know you're a grown woman and you don't have to do as I say. But just consider what it would do to the rest of us if something happened to you. It would destroy our family."

That gave Beck pause. She knew how she would feel if something happened to one of them.

"Okay, Mom. I'll think about it. Really, I will. I'm just going to do a little computer work to wrap up some loose ends. I'll keep it very low key."

"Promise me, Beck, that you'll be careful. Use your good sense."

That was a promise Beck could make. "I'll be careful, Mom. I promise. And I'll use my good sense."

Her mother sighed in resignation. Beck knew she hadn't heard everything she wanted to hear from her daughter. But that was all she was getting from Beck.

"Okay, Beck. Is Lizzie there?"

"Sure. Hold on." Lizzie was across the room, alphabetizing some books that had gotten out of order. Beck handed her the phone, and they switched places.

From hearing Lizzie's side of the conversation, Beck could tell that her mother was urging Lizzie to try to convince her to drop the investigation.

When she hung up, Lizzie walked over to Beck and whispered to her, "Mom wants you to stop, Grammy wants you to stop, but I think you should do what you want to do. Don't let them scare you off!"

Beck couldn't remember ever feeling so much love for her sister.

"But, for now," Lizzie instructed, "will you please go back upstairs and rest? You need to get your strength back." She took Beck by the shoulders and turned her toward the stairs. "I'll bring you up a sandwich."

Beck did feel strangely weak, just from walking downstairs and having a couple of conversations. She couldn't put her finger on it, but maybe it was mental strain. Or too much of an adrenalin rush last night. All she knew was she felt emotionally drained.

So, for the first time in a while, she took her sister's advice. She was beginning to understand, that in her own way, Lizzie was wiser than Beck gave her credit for.

Chapter Thirty-One

Beck did exactly as her sister told her. She ate the shrimp salad sandwich Lizzie carried upstairs for her and flipped through a few pages of *Time* magazine as she lay in bed. The next thing she knew, she woke up in the darkness. Turning her head on her pillow to check the time, she was confused to see her digital clock read 6:14. Why was it dark outside at six o'clock? The realization slowly hit her that it wasn't six at night, but six the next morning. Could she possibly have slept for fourteen hours?

Sitting up in bed, she clicked on her bedside lamp to find a yawning Great Dane on the floor next to the bed, and a mass of curly red hair on the pillow next to hers. Lizzie opened her eyes and stared sleepily at her sister.

"You're up early," Lizzie said.

"Early? I slept for fourteen hours."

"That's good," Lizzie said, closing her eyes again. "You needed it."

Beck gave her dozing sister a bewildered look.

"Why are you in my bed?"

"Protecting you," Lizzie said drowsily. "Coquina, too."

Beck chuckled. She did feel surrounded by her sister and the dog. And she had to say, she did feel safe.

"How long have you been here?" Beck asked. "I didn't hear you come in."

"I came in about eleven. You were dead to the world."

Beck stretched and stood up. Coquina did the same thing.

"What'd you do last night?" Beck asked. "Go out with Teddy?"

"Nope. I told him I needed to stay here to keep an eye on you. He said to tell you he's glad you're okay."

"I don't want you to change your life for me, Lizzie."

Lizzie sat up and rubbed her eyes. "I'm not. I'm just looking out for you for a little while."

Beck nodded. She hadn't expected her sister to be so protective, not that she was complaining. "That's nice," she said. "I appreciate it."

Beck glanced at Coquina who had wandered over to the door and stood staring at it. "Coquina needs to go out. I'll take her."

Lizzie threw off the covers and stood up. "No, I'll take her."

"Lizzie, I can't stay inside the house forever."

"I know. Just for a while longer."

Beck wasn't used to seeing this side of Lizzie. She liked it and wasn't going to turn down her sister's offer to walk the dog. That duty usually fell on Beck.

"Okay, then. If you're sure. Thanks."

"I'm sure."

After Lizzie left with the dog, Beck took a shower and got dressed. When she went into the apartment kitchen, Grammy was already awake, had coffee brewing, and was seated at the table reading the local newspaper.

"You made the front page," her grandmother said, turning around the newspaper for Beck to see.

Beck leaned forward to see her Facebook photo staring back at her under the headline, "Local Bookstore

Owner Survives Murder Attempt." The shooting happened too late at night to make yesterday's newspaper, so here it was a day later.

It was the last thing Beck wanted to see. She valued her privacy and didn't like her picture being splattered across the news. But even more disturbing was the headline of the article next to it: "Lottery Winner Arrested in Tourist Murder."

"They arrested Scratchoff!" she exclaimed. "I can't believe that."

Her grandmother nodded. "I don't know what to think. It says they found the ring in his motel room, as well as bullets that match the one in our front door."

"What!" Beck quickly read the first few paragraphs of the newspaper story. It said, "An anonymous tip led the police to Scratchoff McLean's residence where the valuable emerald ring stolen from a murdered tourist was discovered, along with bullets of the same caliber as the one used in the attempt on a local bookstore owner's life."

"This can't be right," Beck exclaimed. "I'm going down to the police station to talk to Scratchoff. He would never try to shoot me. I know he wouldn't."

"You're going to the police station?" Grammy asked in a startled voice.

"Yes. I want to talk to Scratchoff face to face."

They heard a commotion on the stairs, and Coquina came bounding around the corner. Lizzie was right behind her. Beck could tell from Lizzie's ruddy cheeks and Coquina's sandy paws that she had taken the Great Dane for a run on the beach.

"What's going on," Lizzie asked breathlessly, as she reached in the cabinet for a can of dog food. She picked up Coquina's bowl and set it down on the counter.

Her grandmother held up the newspaper. Lizzie stepped closer and squinted. "Your Facebook picture," she said to Beck. "Looks like you're famous."

"But look at the other headline," Beck told her.

Her sister took hold of the newspaper and read the beginning of the article. "They arrested Scratchoff? Well, if he did it, I'm glad they got him."

"But that's just it, Lizzie," Beck said, taking the newspaper back. "I don't think he did do it."

"Well, the police had evidence," Lizzie said, as she began opening the dog food can with a can opener. "They wouldn't just arrest him for no reason."

"Maybe someone is framing him," Beck speculated. "Maybe someone planted the evidence."

"You mean the real killer?" Lizzie asked.

"Exactly," Beck said. "After breakfast, I'm going down to the jail to visit Scratchoff. I want to hear what he has to say."

"Do you think that's wise, Beck?" Grammy asked. "I'd rather you just stayed inside for a while longer."

Beck put her hands on her hips and glared at her grandmother. "Grammy! Think about it. If Scratchoff is guilty, he's locked up and can't hurt me. If it isn't Scratchoff, the killer isn't going to take the chance of going after me when the police think it is Scratchoff."

Grammy thought about that for a moment. "When you put it that way, it makes sense, I guess."

"The reason you're nervous," Beck told her, "is because down deep, you don't really think Scratchoff is the one. You think the real killer is still out there."

Beck could see by the expression on her grandmother's face that she'd hit the nail on the head. "You're right," her grandmother admitted. "I do still think the killer's still out there."

Lizzie set Coquina's bowl of dogfood on the floor, and the Great Dane enthusiastically began gulping it down.

"Maybe it would be good for you to talk to him in person," Lizzie told her. "Look him in the eye and see if he looks guilty."

Beck hated to ask Lizzie for another favor after everything she'd already done for her but with her picture on the front page, Beck couldn't face the breakfast crowd and all their curious questions. And she wanted to get down to the jail as soon as she could to see Scratchoff.

"Would you mind too much, Lizzie, working breakfast for me? I can't stand the thought of all their questions."

Lizzie nodded. "Sure, I get it. I don't mind. I don't have to be to work today 'til noon."

As soon as they finished breakfast and her grandmother and sister went downstairs to open the bookstore, Beck ran down the back stairs to her car and drove to the two-story stucco police station across the Intracoastal Waterway and about a mile north on U.S. 1.

When she entered the police station and asked to see Scratchoff McLean, the female officer at the desk gave her an odd look. She obviously recognized Beck from that morning's newspaper photo.

Beck waited in the lobby for about fifteen minutes before being led to the small jail in a separate wing behind the police station. She was taken to a small booth with a glass partition between the seats and wall phones on each side. An officer stood behind her until Scratchoff was brought in five minutes later.

Wearing an orange jumpsuit, handcuffed, and in leg irons, Scratchoff was led by a young police officer to the metal chair on the other side of the glass partition from Beck. His hair was wet and slicked back, Beck assumed from a morning shower. Actually, he looked cleaner than she'd ever seen him.

Chapter Thirty-Two

Scratchoff's face erupted into an expression of sheer elation when he saw her, and then his eyes filled with tears.

They both reached for their phones at the same time. "Miss Beck," Scratchoff wailed into the phone. "You have to believe me. I'd never do anything to hurt you. Or that tourist lady neither. Never."

"I do believe you, Scratchoff," she said immediately.

"You do?" It was clear from his stunned expression that he didn't expect that response.

Beck nodded. "I know you'd never do anything to hurt me, Scratchoff."

"Never. I swear on a stack of Bibles." He wiped a tear from his cheek with the back of his hand.

"Tell me what happened, Scratchoff."

"I don't rightly know, Miss Beck. I was just comin' home from ridin' about town as I do, ya know, and the po-lice cars was swarmed in the parking lot. When I come up, that detective feller put me in handcuffs and read me them Mirandy rights."

She could picture Devon enjoying the moment of clapping the cuffs on his murder suspect.

"Why did they arrest you? What did they find in your motel room?"

"They said they found the emerald ring that dead lady had on and some bullets that was the same as the ones that was shot at you. But I ain't never owned no gun, Miss Beck, and I sure never took no ring off no dead tourist lady."

"Do you lock your motel room, Scratchoff?" Beck asked.

He gave her a surprised look. "Well, no, I don't. I was so used to livin' outside in the dunes, that it never occurred to me somebody might want to steal somethin' offa me. I don't have nothin' worth stealin'."

"So, anybody could have gone into your motel room and planted that ring and those bullets?"

Scratchoff eyebrows furrowed into a frown. "I reckon they could have, now that ya mention it. I don't know why anybody would wanna do that to me, though. I never hurt nobody."

Beck's heart went out to Scratchoff. It was obvious to her that someone had framed him. She couldn't imagine how horrible it must feel to be thrown in jail for a crime you didn't commit.

"I'm going to get you out of here, Scratchoff," she told him. "I'm not sure when, but I'm going to find the person who really did this."

Scratchoff teared up again. "Miss Beck, you don't know how much it means to me to hear you say that. You know, you're the first person to ever visit me in jail. That last time when I was here, ya know when they thought I killed those ladies on the beach and I was locked up for two months, nobody visited me. Not one 'cept my public defender. My buddies was too afraid of the po-lice, so they didn't come."

That pulled at Beck's heartstrings. How hard it must have been on him to be wrongly accused and then to have to go through all that by himself.

"How have they been treating you? Good, I hope."

"They're bein' all right, I guess. That new detective feller was nice and polite to me. Called me Mr. McLean when he was handcuffin' me, which I'm not used to hearin'. And the food here's pretty good. The last time I's here, it felt like the food was really good, but I was livin' out in the dunes back then. Now that I got my own place, the food just seems so-so. But I'm doin' all right, I guess."

"I'm glad they're treating you well, Scratchoff. I want you to remember while you're in here, that I know you're innocent."

He still seemed a bit astonished that she was on his side. "Really, Miss Beck? Even though they said I's the one that shot at ya?"

"I don't believe that for a second, Scratchoff."

He started to tear up again. "Miss Beck, you're like an angel from heaven."

"You stay strong, Scratchoff. I'm going to get you out of here soon." She hung up the phone, stood up, and waved goodbye as the guard came over to take him back to his cell.

He looked so sad and pathetic. She was used to seeing his ebullient personality, so full of life. Yes, Scratchoff was odd. And he definitely could be annoying. No doubt about that. But, so what? He was part of their community and had been for a long time. And he had done a really good thing setting up the motel to help other homeless people. He could have been selfish with the money he won and bought a big house and a fancy car, like most people probably would have done. But he didn't. She didn't think he even owned a car. Just that beach bike. She would never believe that he had taken a shot at her.

When she left the visiting area and entered the lobby of the police station, Devon approached her. She figured someone had tipped him off that she was here, and he had been waiting for her.

"How are you doing, Beck?" he asked. "Feeling better?"

"I'm just fine, thanks," she answered curtly. She couldn't help adding, "I can't believe you actually think Scratchoff McLean had anything to do with killing Peggy Davidson and shooting at me."

He flinched at her statement. "Well, that's definitely not the response I was expecting."

"If you're looking for a thank you, you won't get one from me. You arrested the wrong man."

"Beck," he said pointedly, "We found the emerald ring and bullets that matched the gun that shot at you in his motel room."

“Wasn’t that convenient?” Beck asked sarcastically. “It’s so obvious that he was set up.”

Devon seemed taken aback. He put his hands on his hips and stared at her. “Why would you say that?”

Beck let out a long sigh. “Look, Devon, you’re new in town. Those of us who have lived here a long time know Scratchoff, and we know he’s not a killer. Someone obviously planted that evidence in his motel room.”

Devon shook his head and pursed his lips. “Beck, I’m not going to argue with you. You can believe what you want to believe, but we’ve got evidence to back up our theories. I thought you’d be happy we arrested the person who tried to kill you.”

“I would have been happy if you’d arrested the right person,” she retorted.

She was amazed at herself. Proud of herself. She no longer felt any degree of intimidation from this man that used to evoke such girlish emotion from her.

“Did you ever find the brick?” she asked him. “I’d be willing to bet you anything that you didn’t find Scratchoff’s fingerprints on the brick.”

Devon didn’t back down. “The brick never turned up. We’re sure it’s where everything else is that we can never find—at the bottom of the ocean.”

"I'm not surprised. Not in the least."

He shook his head in exasperation. "Beck, honestly. We know what we're doing."

"Look, Devon, I'm not going to argue with you," she said in a challenging tone. "But I'm going to prove you wrong."

He took hold of her arm. "Beck, would you please be careful? A lot of people don't like it when somebody starts nosing around in their life."

Beck shrugged. "If you're so sure you have the right killer in jail, I should have nothing to worry about."

With that, she turned her back on him and strode away. She couldn't resist a quick peek back and saw Devon still standing in the same place with his hands on his hips, gazing after her.

Chapter Thirty-Three

Since Beck was already away from the bookstore with her car and had some extra time before she needed to be back, there was another stop she wanted to make. Something had been nagging at her since her trip to Palm Beach.

The largest real estate firm in the area was two miles down the road, and one of Beach Reads regular customers was one of the most knowledgeable real estate minds in the area. Even Grammy paid attention when Angie Miller spoke about the real estate market, which was saying something.

Beck took a chance that Angie would be in and not out showing property to clients. She was in luck.

"Beck," the real estate broker said with concern after being called up to the lobby by the receptionist. "I read about you in the paper this morning. What a scare you had. Are you all right?"

"Hi Angie," Beck said. "I guess I got lucky. Do you have a minute?"

"Sure," Angie said, waving for Beck to follow her to her office. They talked about Beck's harrowing escape from a bullet two nights before as they walked back to her office. After they both sat down, Angie asked her, "What brings you in, Beck?"

"It's about SeaBreeze Point," Beck told her. "I have a friend who's thinking of investing in it. Do you think it's a good investment?"

"Hmm," the real broker responded, lifting an eyebrow. "I don't like to talk negatively about any projects in our area, but just between you and me, you might want to guide them away from that one. It's been fraught with problems—zoning, foundation work, environmental issues, not to mention cash flow. I'd hate to see your friend throw good money after bad."

Beck nodded. She sensed that might be the case. "I met the developer's wife the other day down in Palm Beach. What a beautiful place they have."

Angie grimaced. "I hope they're able to hang onto it. Again, confidentially, I hear Palmer's mortgaged it to the hilt to bankroll SeaBreeze Point."

No wonder Beck didn't see any servants at the huge estate, and the grounds look a little shaggy, not immaculate like most of their neighbors. She hoped for Lenora's sake that they didn't lose the house.

"That's all I was wondering about, Angie," Beck said, standing up. "I won't take any more of your time. Thanks for the information."

"I'm sorry for what you've been going through, Beck," Angie told her as she walked her back out to the lobby. "I had planned to come to the book signing that night the tourist was murdered, but I ended up having a late showing. I'm so glad they caught the culprit."

Beck shrugged. "I'm not so sure they have the right person, Angie."

"Really? The police sure made it sound that way in the paper."

Beck was relieved when the receptionist interrupted them. "Angie, call on line three."

"Thanks again, Angie," Beck said with a wave, as Angie hurried back to her office to take the call.

Interesting, Beck thought, as she drove back to the bookstore, though she wasn't surprised. She wondered just how much the developer Jordan Palmer needed the influx of funds into his problematic SeaBreeze Point development from Joe Davidson. Peggy Davidson was dead set against the investment. Now she was dead. Had she been in Jordan Palmer's way?

The skies had darkened, and it started to drizzle as Beck left the real estate office. By the time she arrived back at the bookstore, it was pouring. When she dashed through the kitchen door into the bookstore, she was surprised to find Joe and Lisa Davidson seated at a table eating Grammy's chicken salad sandwiches. Grammy was hovering over them, and Lizzie was at the cash register checking out another customer.

"There's poor Beck," Lisa cried solicitously, rising to give Beck a hug. Beck wasn't sure how to react. Lisa was still near the top of her suspect list.

"I'm okay. Really," Beck said. They bombarded her with questions about the shooting, and she answered as best she could, assuring them she was fine. They couldn't understand why she was targeted, but Beck just shrugged it off. If they hadn't figured out she was snooping around into their backgrounds, she certainly wasn't going to tell them.

"What a traumatic experience," Joe said consolingly. "We're so glad the police have arrested the person responsible. It'll make our trip home much easier knowing my mother's killer has been captured."

"Your trip back?" Beck said, avoiding discussion of the arrest. "You're leaving?"

"The police are releasing the body and told us that since they made the arrest, we're free to go back to North Carolina. We're flying out tomorrow afternoon from West Palm," Joe told her.

"Oh. I'm so sorry to see you go," she said. Not only had she grown to like the couple, Joe in particular, but she also wasn't finished investigating them. She had some real suspicions about Lisa and her brother. "And your brother? Will he go back, too?"

"No, he went back to Ft. Lauderdale to continue his job search," Lisa said.

Grammy spoke up. "I was just telling them that we sure will miss them here."

"But we very well may be back in the next few months, and maybe permanently," Joe told them. "I'm strongly considering investing in SeaBreeze Point, and we may make a home there."

Beck couldn't keep quiet about the investment but chose her words carefully. "Joe, I know you're enthusiastic about the development, but you may want to do more vetting before you decide to invest. I understand that development has run into a number of problems."

"Don't worry, Beck. I'll do solid research before I spend the kind of money they want me to invest," Joe said.

Beck hated to see him get involved in a bad deal, even though he now had all the money in the world to invest. "You might want to talk to Angie Miller," she suggested. "She's the most savvy real estate pro in town."

Beck dug into her purse and found the card she'd picked up off the real estate broker's desk. "Here's her card."

"Angie Miller really is on top of things," Grammy assured them. "She knows what's going on."

"Well, thank you, then," Joe responded, tucking the card into his shirt pocket. "I'll be sure to give her a ring."

They stood to leave, shared hugs all around, and Grammy told them she hoped to see them back in Manatee Beach again soon. Beck had a whole different mindset. They're not leaving until tomorrow afternoon, she thought. She still had time to find out everything she could about them today.

Chapter Thirty-Four

"Thanks for covering for me, Lizzie," Beck told her sister after the store cleared out. Grammy came to the cash register to join them.

"No problem," Lizzie said. "I couldn't work today anyway with the rain, and I made some tips. So, it's all good. I didn't mind at all"

"How was Scratchoff?" Grammy asked.

"Oh, Grammy. I felt so sorry for him. He looked so lost and pathetic. Even if I hadn't believed he was innocent before, I really do now."

"Well, if he didn't do it," Lizzie asked, "who do you think did?"

"I'm not sure," Beck said. "But there are other people out there who had a lot stronger motive than Scratchoff did."

Beck needed some serious time on the computer. There were so many details she wanted to research further, in particular about Jordan Palmer, as well as Lisa and her brother. The downpour outside might have been her salvation. The store didn't do much business when the weather was like this, and Lizzie didn't have to go to her lifeguard job. She'd be on call if the weather cleared up, but Beck had seen in the newspaper that it was supposed to rain the rest of the day. So maybe Lizzie wouldn't mind covering for her a little longer.

The bookstore had emptied out as people ran for their cars through the downpour. Beck knew it would be a slow afternoon.

"Look, I hate to ask you for anything more, Lizzie, but I need to do some computer work on the investigation. Do you think you could cover for me for a while longer?"

Grammy answered for her. "We're not going to have any customers in this rain anyway. You two go ahead. I'll cover the store just in case somebody comes in."

Relieved, Beck immediately went upstairs to her bedroom and shut the door. Sitting down at her desk, she opened her desktop and spent the next hour pouring over every article she could find about SeaBreeze Point and

Jordan Palmer. By the time she was finished, it was clear to her how desperate Palmer was for funds to get his stalled SeaBreeze Point development moving forward again. She wondered just how much receiving a huge investment from Joe Davidson meant to Jordan Palmer, and what he was willing to do to get it.

Next, Beck turned her attention to Lisa and Eric Jones. She tried several different approaches, but couldn't find anything on Lisa Jones. Nothing. It was as if the woman didn't exist before she married Joe Davidson. So, she moved on to focus on Eric Jones. Peggy Davidson had suspected he might have a criminal record, and, despite his common name, Beck was determined to find out if she was right. He had been living in North Carolina, too, though she wasn't sure about which city. This might take some time. Everything would be so much simpler if she just had their birthdates, or their last known addresses. But she was working in the dark. The cops had it easy, and if she were on better terms with Devon, she would have asked him to look up some of the information she needed. But as it was—

Lizzie appeared at her bedroom door. "Are you busy?"

Beck glanced up from her laptop and stretched. She pushed her chair away from the desk. “Never too busy for you, Lizzie. What’s up?”

Lizzie took a flying leap and lay sprawled face down across her sister’s bed. “Ugh,” she moaned.

Beck was used to Lizzie’s histrionics so she wasn’t overly concerned. “What’s wrong, Lizzie?”

Lizzie rolled over and stared at the ceiling. “I’ve decided to break up with Teddy.”

That was a surprise. Beck thought they were getting along great. “Aww. How come? I like Teddy.”

“That’s the problem. I like him, too. But that doesn’t mean I want to see him every single day.”

Beck had heard her sister complain about the same thing with other boys she’d dated. “Have you told him you need your space?”

Lizzie rolled on her side, leaned her head on her fist, and stared at her sister. “I’ve tried to, but it just doesn’t seem to be getting through. He’s not the only thing I have going on in my life.”

“That’s probably the problem,” Beck told her. “You’re the only thing going on in his.”

Lizzie grimaced. “It’s starting to really get on my nerves. He keeps bugging me to get together when I really don’t feel like it. He’s getting way too clingy.”

“Sometimes I think we O’Rourke girls are too independent for our own good,” Beck said, a wistful note entering her voice.

“Bite your tongue!” Lizzie scolded. “The guys just need to man up!”

Beck realized Lizzie was right, of course. In matters concerning men, Lizzie always seemed to have her head on straight.

“Well, at least Teddy lasted a week. Nearly two,” Beck said.

Lizzie shrugged. “I’m nineteen, for God’s sake. I’m not looking for a husband. I just want somebody to hang out with sometimes. Why can’t men understand that?”

Beck laughed. “You’re asking the wrong person. I don’t have a clue.”

Lizzie rolled over on her back and stared at the ceiling. “He’s coming over tonight about seven. I’m going to tell him then.”

Beck nodded. That was her cue to make herself scarce. It seemed that every couple of weeks, the living room was off-limits to Beck and Grammy while Lizzie gave her latest boyfriend the bad news.

"Okay, I'll stay in my room. I think Grammy said she's going to Dorothy's for dinner. So, you'll have the living room to yourselves."

"Thanks," Lizzie said, sitting up. "It won't take long. I hope not, anyway."

Beck found herself feeling sorry for Teddy, sorrier than she had for most of Lizzie's other past discards. "Well, be kind. Remember, he's alone in the world. No parents, no brothers and sisters."

"I'm always kind!" Lizzie said defensively. "I always tell them I want to stay friends. And I mean it. I do want to stay friends."

"Let's hope he does, too."

"There are lots of other girl fishies in the sea, too. Teddy's so cute, I'm sure it won't take him long to find somebody who's as needy as he is."

"Well, when you put it that way," Beck replied with a chuckle, "I don't feel as bad for him."

Lizzie glanced at her sister's laptop. "How's the research coming? Found the killer yet?"

Beck shook her head. "Slowly. It's starting to give me a headache. I'm going to take a break and then get back to it later. I was thinking of making spaghetti for dinner. How does that sound?"

"Sure. I love your spaghetti."

Beck glanced out the window. The rain was still coming down in torrents. "Okay. How about dinner at six? That'll give you time to get ready for Teddy."

"Works for me."

Chapter Thirty-Five

The rainstorm continued all afternoon, so Grammy decided to close the store early. They hadn't had a customer since three o'clock. Streams of rainwater slid down the sidewalk in front of the store, as well as down the side alley. Lightening came and went, and thunder grumbled in the distance most of the afternoon.

"Is that spaghetti sauce I smell?" Grammy asked cheerily when she reached the top of the landing. The strong aroma of garlic and oregano permeated the apartment.

Beck poked her head out of the kitchen, oven mitts on both hands. "It sure is. But I guess you're going to have to miss out since you're going to Dorothy's for dinner."

Grammy shook her head. “Oh, no. Not anymore. I’m not about to go out in this weather for anything. We’re going to do it later this week.”

“Well, good then. I made plenty. It’ll be ready in about ten minutes.”

When they sat down for dinner at the small table in the kitchen, Beck announced to Grammy that Lizzie would be needing the living room that night at seven.

Her grandmother knew immediately what that meant. “Aww. Darn it! I like Teddy. He’s been a lot of help around here.”

Lizzie pursed her lips and frowned. “I know, Grammy, but being a lot of help around the house isn’t exactly what I’m looking for in a boyfriend.”

“It will be someday,” Grammy retorted.

“Maybe. But it’s not now.”

“Okay, okay. Who am I to argue?” Grammy replied. “My quiz shows are on then, so I will happily vacate to the bedroom.”

“Thanks, Grammy.”

After dinner, Lizzie helped with the clean-up, so they all went their separate ways about six-thirty. Grammy trotted off to her bedroom and shut the door. Beck heard the television set come on.

Lizzie left to get ready for Teddy's visit, and when Beck finished in the kitchen, she went into her bedroom and closed the door. She let out a long sigh and sat down again at the computer. All this research was making her weary, but she needed to forge on.

Sick of searching for information on the Joneses, she decided to take another tack. Picking up her legal pad, she flipped back to the notes she had taken when she talked to Janie Foster. She typed in the name of the small town where Peggy Davidson lived not far from Kitty Hawk. Hawk's Cove.

Peggy had so much death in the past couple of years. That's what Janie had said. Her next-door neighbor fell off a ladder and broke his neck a couple of days before she left for Florida. Beck found the small weekly newspaper of the town, the Cove Courier, and there was the story. The poor man was only fifty-five years old and had been cleaning his gutters. The sheriff's office believed the family's Golden Retriever had bumped into the ladder. How tragic.

Beck continued to flip through past issues of the newspaper, looking for something, anything, that might give her a clue to someone who might have wanted Peggy Davidson dead.

She heard the doorbell downstairs and glanced at her watch. Seven o'clock. Poor Teddy. He'd had to come out in this horrible weather just to be dumped on his head. Oh well. A nice kid like that was sure to rebound quickly. That's just the way romance was at that age.

Going back to her online search, she heard muffled voices in the living room a couple of minutes later. As she continued to scroll through past issues of the newspaper, a headline caught her eye. "Still No Arrests in Arson Deaths." Arson? Didn't Janie say one of Peggy Davidson's best friends and her husband were killed in a fire?

Beck clicked on the article and a photo of an attractive couple, probably ten years younger than Peggy, appeared on the screen. What a shame, she thought. They'd both perished in a fire of their oceanfront home that the police believed was started by their teenage son. Apparently, the son had cleared out their bank accounts and dropped out of sight. The police had been searching for him for nearly two years to no avail.

Something nagged at her about the story. She couldn't quite put her finger on it, but she wanted to know more. She typed in the name of the couple who died in the fire, Baker. Several articles popped up. She went back to the earlier ones from nearly two years before.

The article described the couple's troubled teenage son, Edward Baker, Jr. The police had been called to the house several times after he'd threatened his mother and gotten violent with her. His parents were considering sending him away to military school when the fire erupted. As she scrolled down the page, an image of the son began to appear. It looked like a high school photograph. First his black hair, then his handsome teenage face, complete with a beaming smile and adorable dimples. A really cute kid. Not the face you'd expect to see of a suspected killer.

It took Beck a moment to realize who she was looking at. He was younger, and the hair threw her off. But the first words out of her mouth when she realized who she was looking at were, "He dyed it." And suddenly she knew what Peggy Davidson meant by the last thing she said right before she ran out of the bookstore that night. Not, "He died," but "He dyed." Teddy had dyed his dark hair, peroxided it light blond.

It all became clear to Beck. Teddy had been in the bookstore that night helping them rearrange the furniture after the book signing. Peggy was standing next to the cash register talking to Marcia Graybill's husband, and Teddy was moving chairs right in front of her. They must have made eye contact at some point, and she recognized Teddy, the son of her dear friend. She probably panicked and hurried out of the store to find her son. No doubt, Teddy followed her. He couldn't afford for his secret to get out. There were so many people in the store at that time, it would have been easy for him to slip out, kill his mother's friend, and then slip back in. He was probably only gone for four or five minutes.

And Teddy had been in the store when they talked about Scratchoff and how the police suspected him of killing Peggy Davidson to steal her ring. He'd acted like he wasn't paying attention, but undoubtedly, he was. How easy it would have been for him to follow Scratchoff home, wait for him to leave, and then slip into his motel room to plant the emerald ring and the bullets.

The bullets. The hair on the back of her neck rose and her heart rate took off. Teddy, who knew she was investigating Peggy Davidson's background and might come across his name. Teddy, who took a shot at her, and might have killed her if she hadn't bent down to pick up a piece of paper. Teddy, who right now was in the living room with her sister.

Chapter Thirty-Six

Her phone. Where was her phone? She needed to call Devon to get the police over here right away. Pushing away the papers scattered across the desk, she searched for her cell phone. Not there. She grabbed her purse and quickly searched it. Finding nothing, she turned it upside down. But still no phone.

She jumped up and ran to her nightstand. That's where she usually kept it at night. Maybe she'd automatically set it down there. But it wasn't there, either. She looked on the floor next to the nightstand and even got down on her hands and knees to check under the bed. But she couldn't find the cell phone. She tried to think. Patting her pockets to be sure it wasn't there, she tried to remember when she'd used the phone last. Finally, it came to her. She'd had it in the kitchen with her when she was cooking. Now, she remembered. She'd been checking her email while she waited for the pasta to boil. It was on the kitchen counter, next to the toaster.

Should she send an email to Devon from her laptop? The problem with that was, people didn't always read their email right away, and she didn't have his email address anyway. It would take time to look it up, and in the meantime, her sister was in the midst of breaking up with a killer—a very disturbed young man who had killed his parents and tried to shoot her. The first thing she needed to do was to protect her sister.

She wished she could get to Grammy's room to use her phone, but she'd have to cross the living room to do that. Beck opened her door a sliver. Teddy had his back to her on the couch. Coquina lay on the floor, blocking her path to the kitchen. Her only option, she decided, was to nonchalantly walk past them to the kitchen, grab her phone, and then return to the bedroom to call the police. As far as Coquina blocking her path, she'd either have to step over the dog or shoo her out of the way.

Beck slid quietly out of her bedroom and stopped to listen for a moment. In the distance, she heard the wheel turning on Grammy's favorite game show in her bedroom. In the living room, she heard her sister say two words that she knew could mean trouble, "I'm sorry."

Beck decided to make her move. What other choice did she have? Who knew how someone like Teddy would react to being rejected? She opened her bedroom door and tiptoed quietly across the living room toward the kitchen. "Move, Coquina," she whispered, touching the dog on its back. The Great Dane jumped to her feet.

Lizzie looked up at Beck in surprise, and Teddy followed her gaze.

"Don't mind me," she said quickly. "I just need to get something in the kitchen."

But something in her wary eyes must have tipped off Teddy.

"You're the reason for this, aren't you?" he accused Beck, his voice bitter. "You and your little amateur investigation."

Teddy stood up and took a step toward her. Beck backed away, still trying to get past the dog to the kitchen. "I don't have anything to do with it, Teddy," she told him.

Lizzie sat up in alarm. "What are you talking about? What's going on?"

Teddy glared at Lizzie. "You're breaking up with me because of her, because of her stupid investigation."

Beck couldn't believe the extent of Teddy's paranoia. She didn't think she'd given herself away, but just seeing her while he was going through the emotional turmoil of the breakup must have set him off.

Lizzie gave him a perplexed frown. "No, Teddy. It's what I told you. I just need more space. I'm not ready for a relationship."

He sneered at her, the gentle teenage luster gone. "Yeah, right, Lizzie. Admit it. You're afraid of me. Your sister has filled your head with all kinds of lies about me."

Puzzled, Lizzie said, "I don't know what you're talking about, Teddy." She started to stand up from the couch, but Teddy pulled a gun out of his pocket.

"Teddy!" Lizzie shrieked. "What are you doing?"

He came around behind Lizzie, wrapped his arm around her neck, and put the gun to her head.

"Teddy!" Lizzie yelled again. "You'll meet somebody else. You'll see."

Beck's heart leapt to her throat, but she tried to calm herself. Coquina started barking at Teddy and didn't stop. The big dog looked like she might attack him.

"Get that dog away from me or I'll shoot it," he screamed at Beck.

Terrified, Beck knelt down, took the dog by the collar, and hugged her, trying to quiet her down. "Shh. Quiet, Coquina. Shh."

Beck looked up into her sister's frightened eyes.

"I don't understand," Lizzie cried. "Why is this happening?"

"This is about more than your break up, Lizzie," Beck said, trying to distract Teddy. "Teddy is the murderer I've been searching for."

Lizzie's eyes flashed in horror. She tried to look sideways at his face, but he held her firmly with his arm across her throat.

"Teddy?" Lizzie cried. "No. That's impossible."

Frightened to her core, Beck spoke with a bravado she didn't feel. "Peggy Davidson recognized you, didn't she, Teddy? Even with your peroxided white hair, she recognized you as the son who set his parent's house on fire."

"You think you're so smart," Teddy said, wagging his gun toward the kitchen. "Get in there."

Beck stood up and started moving slowly toward the kitchen. Coquina, calmer now, followed her. But Beck didn't stop talking. "And you knew your mother's close friend would turn you in, so you followed her out of the bookstore, beat her with a brick, and then dragged her body to the back alley."

"I did no such thing," Teddy retorted, pushing Lizzie toward the kitchen.

"Oh, yes, you did. Lizzie, I'll bet if you think back, you'll remember that Teddy disappeared for a while after the book signing."

An expression of shock had settled onto Lizzie's face, but she appeared to be trying to remember. "You were gone for a few minutes," she said after a few moments, with a frown. She tried to turn her head to talk to him, but she couldn't move. "When I asked you where you were, you said you were taking out the garbage. But later, the garbage was still there. I remember thinking, 'I thought he took it out already.'"

"Just shut up, both of you." He pointed the gun at Beck when they reached the kitchen. "Turn on the stove."

Beck froze as the realization hit her of what he planned to do. "No. I'm not doing that. I'm not going to let you burn down our house, too."

"Do it or I'll shoot her," Teddy threatened, holding the gun at Lizzie's head.

Lizzie's eyes grew large but she shouted at her sister, "No, Beck, don't."

"I said turn on the stove." He cocked the gun at Lizzie's head.

Beck held up her hands. "Okay, okay. I'll turn on the stove."

She reached out and turned on one of the burners.

He nodded toward a roll of paper towels on the counter. "Pick up those paper towels."

Beck frowned and hesitated, trying to think of a way to stop him. Behind him, she caught a flicker of movement and realized Grammy was creeping up holding a glass vase with both hands over her head.

Beck tried to distract him as she reached out for the roll of paper towels by saying, "And then you tried to shoot me. Too bad I ducked at just the right time."

"Shut up and light that paper, or I won't miss this time."

Suddenly, Grammy brought the glass vase slamming down onto the back of his head. It didn't knock Teddy out, but it stunned him. As he loosened his grip on Lizzie to turn to take a shot at Grammy, Lizzie elbowed him in the stomach, reached behind her, grabbed him around the neck, and flipped him over her shoulder, a move Beck had seen her practice in lifeguard training.

Teddy lay sprawled across the floor, blood dripping from his head. The gun went flying across the kitchen floor.

Beck jumped forward, grabbed the gun, and pointed it at Teddy.

"Don't move!" she ordered him. "Trust me. I'm a better shot than you are."

Lizzie lifted a foot and stepped hard onto his stomach. "You should know better than to mess with the O'Rourke women."

A moment later, they heard police sirens.

"I called 911 from the bedroom," Grammy told them. "They made good time."

Chapter Thirty-Seven

They heard the front door downstairs crash open, and before they had time to react, several police officers, guns drawn, rushed into the kitchen. Devon was right behind them.

Two officers dragged Teddy to his feet and handcuffed his hands behind his back. Shaking his peroxided hair out of his eyes, Teddy gave Beck one last scowl before they led him out of the room. Beck heard Teddy being quoted his Miranda rights by the officers as they led him down the stairs.

Devon stood in front of the three women with his hands on hips and a puzzled look on his face.

"What in the world happened here?"

"He was going to burn down our house," Lizzie told him breathlessly. "He had a gun to my head. Grammy hit him with a vase, I flipped him over, and Beck grabbed the gun."

"And Coquina alerted me by barking," Grammy said. "So, it was a total team effort."

Devon nodded, impressed. He said with a chuckle, "Looks like somebody messed with the wrong family."

He stepped toward Beck and took hold of the gun she held by her side. "I'll take that now," he said.

She handed it to him. "I think you'll find that gun matches the bullet that was shot at me, as well as those you found in Scratchoff's McLean's motel room."

Devon frowned, a perplexed expression settling onto his face.

"What makes you think that?"

Feeling drained of all her energy, Beck slumped into a kitchen chair and gestured for Devon to take a seat, too. Lizzie and Grammy sat down with them. Devon took out his notepad and jotted down notes as they spoke.

"Teddy, the boy your officers just arrested, was Lizzie's boyfriend," Beck began.

"Not anymore," Lizzie interrupted. "I just broke up with him."

"Right," Beck continued. "What we didn't know until I just discovered it online tonight, is that Teddy is actually Edward Baker, Jr. He's been on the run from North Carolina police for nearly two years for setting fire to his house and killing his parents. He also emptied out their bank account."

"I can't believe Teddy did that," Lizzie exclaimed, burying her face in her hands. "How could I have dated someone so horrible. He was always so sweet to me."

"You have nothing to be ashamed of Lizzie," Beck told her. "I think Teddy legitimately liked you. People like him are only dangerous when they're crossed or threatened. They can be real charmers—the last person anyone would suspect."

"I sure never would have suspected him," Grammy said. "I liked him better than any boyfriend Lizzie's ever had."

Devon shifted uncomfortably. "Actually, I've heard the name. He's on the ten most wanted list. Beachside police departments have been told to be on the lookout for him because he supposedly was some kind of a junior surfing champion back in North Carolina."

"No wonder he was so good," Lizzie said. "I didn't know he was from North Carolina, though. We never talked about it. I just figured he was from Florida."

"I'm sure he kept that from you, Lizzie," Grammy told her. "He wouldn't have wanted you to know he was from North Carolina."

Beck nodded in agreement and then continued. "Teddy's mother was a close friend of Peggy Davidson's. Teddy came in after the book signing was over to help us rearrange the furniture. Peggy must have recognized him. He realized it, and followed her when she left and killed her."

"Why is this the first time I'm hearing about Teddy?" Devon asked with a frown. "I don't remember his name being mentioned as someone who was at the book signing."

Beck traded a look with Grammy. "Didn't we mention him?"

Grammy shrugged. "Maybe not. He kind of felt like one of the family. It didn't occur to me."

Beck gave Devon a sideways glance. "Sorry. He came in later to help out, and it just didn't occur to us since he didn't actually attend the book signing."

Devon pursed his lips. Beck could see he was annoyed. But all he said was, "Go on."

"Lizzie remembers now that he was missing for a few minutes after the book signing. He said he was outside taking out the garbage, but the garbage hadn't been taken out. Right, Lizzie?"

"Yeah. I remember looking around for him, wondering where he'd gone."

"He was in such a rush," Beck continued, "that he just hit Peggy, dragged her body behind the building, and probably grabbed the ring as an afterthought, to make it look like a robbery. From what I read, he didn't need the money because he stole so much from his parents. But he knew the Davidsons, and I'm sure he knew that ring was really valuable. He didn't have time to do much else because he knew he would be missed at the bookstore."

Lizzie was still stunned that she had been dating a murderer. "I can't believe Teddy went outside and did that. Then he came back in like nothing happened. We went upstairs and watched TV."

Beck shook her head. "He had us all fooled, Lizzie. He just seemed like such a nice guy."

"I wonder what he would have done after I broke up with him if you hadn't found out who he was?" Lizzie asked.

"I hate to think about it, Lizzie," Beck said, "but he probably would have left and then come back when we were asleep and burned the house down. He wanted me out of the way, and if he was angry at you, too—that seems to be the way he took care of people he didn't want around."

"Oh, my God," Lizzie said, with a shiver.

Devon eyed Beck sternly. "I'm glad everything turned out for the best, but I told you it was dangerous snooping around when there's a murderer on the loose. Especially if the murderer realizes you're on to him."

Beck glanced at Devon sheepishly. She was well aware he didn't approve of her investigating on her own. "Teddy only found out because he was around all the time with Lizzie. I guess he was afraid I'd come across him in my research."

Devon leaned back in his chair and crossed his arms. "Research, huh?" His voice had a scolding tone, but with a sense of amusement to it.

Beck shrugged and sent him a half-smile. "I just felt very strongly that because of the way the victim was killed, that someone from her past probably had it in for her for some reason or another." She added, glancing away from him as she said it, "I just didn't think robbery was the main motive." That was as close as she came to saying, "I told you so."

When she stole a look at him, he was standing, flipping his notebook shut. "Okay," he said, walking toward the door. "You've given me a lot to look into."

He stopped and glanced back at them. "The main thing is, three of my favorite ladies in Manatee Beach are safe. And, I have to say, I'm very impressed."

Coquina chose that moment to jump up and place her front paws on the kitchen table.

"Oh, excuse me," Devon said with a laugh. "Four of my favorite ladies."

Chapter Thirty-Eight

Beck certainly wasn't expecting it, but the phone rang nonstop that night. First, it was the local *Manatee Beach Journal*, next it was the *Miami Herald,* then it was the *Palm Beach Post*. Apparently, the arrest of Edward Baker, Jr., was very big news. And the fact that three women from the same family had been able to trip him up and turn him in to the police, made it even bigger.

The next two days were a whirlwind. Two Miami television stations and CNN interviewed the three of them, and *People* magazine even sent a reporter for an interview. Several newspapers in North Carolina called and a couple of them sent reporters. Detective Devon Mathis had been kind, even gracious, in his praise of the three O'Rourke women, in particular Beck, for solving the murder of the tourist from North Carolina and capturing the longtime fugitive from justice, Edward Baker, Jr.

Before they left Manatee Beach the next afternoon, Joe and Lisa Davidson stopped by Beach Reads to check on Beck and her grandmother and to thank them for capturing the real murderer.

"I remember Eddie Baker very well," Joe told them. "I spent several evenings at their house before the tragedy. I can't believe he's been hiding out down here all that time."

"I know," Beck said. "I guess he took the name Teddy since it was so close to his real name."

Lizzie was standing by listening. "You knew him, too?" she asked Joe. "I just thought of something. That night when you came to dinner at our house, Teddy was supposed to come over and pick me up. But after I told him about the dinner, he said he was having car trouble and asked me to pick him up instead. He must have been afraid you'd see him."

"I'll bet you're right," Joe said. "Eddie is very smart but very dangerous. His parents were such nice people. Nobody could believe what he did. I'm just glad you and your family came out of this unscathed."

Lisa had kind words for Beck before they left town. "You have no idea how much it means to my husband to know what really happened to his mother. I can't thank you enough."

Beck wondered how Lisa would feel if she knew that she and her brother were at the top of Beck's suspect list. Now, she felt a little bad about misjudging her, especially when she saw how caring Lisa was about Joe's welfare.

"I'm so glad we got to know you both. I just wish it had been under better circumstances," Beck told her.

"You may be seeing us again. My brother has decided to join the Coast Guard and hopes to be stationed in Ft. Lauderdale," Lisa told her. "So, we'll be down for visits. And who knows? We may end up buying down here."

"We'd love it if you moved here," Grammy told them.

"If we do, I want to get involved in volunteer work," Lisa said, squeezing her husband's hand. "Seeing all the good that my mother-in-law was able to do, I want to follow in her footsteps." Joe's eyes lit up at his wife's comment.

When they got ready to leave, Joe gave Beck a long hug. "You'll never know how much what you've done has helped me. I feel like I have some closure now."

Being able to find the real killer to give Peggy Davidson's son some peace, meant the world to Beck, too. She finally felt like she could let go of some of the guilt she'd been feeling.

Later that day, the O'Rourkes received another visitor. They heard him before they saw him. "I'm free! I'm free!" he chanted, as he pedaled his bike to their front door. An exuberant Scratchoff McLean, back to his normal appearance of tangled hair, cutoff jeans, wrinkled tank top, and flipflops, rushed into the bookstore and hugged all three of the women. A look of panic like Beck had never seen crossed Lizzie's face as she quickly broke his embrace and stepped away from him.

"You ladies saved my life, you sure did," Scratchoff gushed. "Miss Beck, I don't know how I'll ever thank you. Those po-lice wouldn't listen to a word I said."

"We knew you were innocent all along, Scratchoff," Beck told him. "There was never a doubt in our minds."

"I'm so happy. I'm feelin' lucky. I'm gonna go buy me lots of scratch-off tickets and, Miss Beck, I'm gonna give you half of everythin' I win."

Beck thanked him for the offer but told him no. "You keep whatever you win, Scratchoff. You deserve it after what you've been through."

"How 'bout you, Miss Alice. Will you take half of my winnings?"

Grammy looked tempted, and thought about it for several moments. But she turned him down, too. "No," she said, "I'm just glad you're out of jail. I hope you hit big because you never should have been locked up in the first place."

"You knowed I was innocent the whole time, too, didn't ya, Miss Alice?"

Grammy gave him a sly smile. "You may have a few screws loose, Scratchoff, but I knew you weren't a murderer."

His jovial expression disappeared for a second, but then he broke into a wide smile. "I know you're just joshing with me, Miss Alice, 'cause that's what friends do. And you've got a good friend in me from here on out. You're gonna be seein' a lot more of me around here."

As he rode off on his bike, waving wildly at them and starting his "I'm free" chant again, Grammy and Beck exchanged horrified glances and then burst out laughing. "What have we done?" Grammy exclaimed.

"See more of him? We see way too much of him already."

Beck also received an unexpected phone call from Marcia Graybill. She couldn't imagine why the author was calling her.

"Beck, dear," Marcia Graybill's singsong voice rang out over the phone. "You're all over the news! I'm so glad you're safe and that you were able to catch the culprit. Well done. Very Annabelle of you."

Beck laughed at the reference to the author's heroine. "Well, thank you, Ms. Graybill. It was pretty touch and go there for a while."

"My husband and I talked about it after you called us and got quite a laugh that we were actually on your suspect list. I guess I should take it as a compliment."

Beck felt her face flush. She realized she'd been pretty transparent in her telephone conversation with the author's husband. She decided to make light of it.

"Just like Annabelle, I left no stone unturned. But I never seriously suspected—"

"Oh, my dear, Beck," Ms. Graybill interrupted, "I would have lost all respect for you if I wasn't among your suspects. Those girls were so nasty to me in high school, I felt like bludgeoning them many times."

Beck wasn't quite sure what to say to that. But she didn't have to worry, because the author continued talking without taking a breath. "I learned a long time ago, though, that the best revenge is success. And I think I've done quite a good job of that, don't you, dear?"

Beck smiled to herself. She'd gotten used to Marcia Graybill's voracious ego. "Absolutely. You definitely showed them."

"Well, I'm at the airport now on my way to Dallas for another signing, but I just had to call to congratulate you. And I wanted to let you know I'll be back at your bookstore next spring for a signing of my new book, as yet unnamed. I told my publisher to put you at the top of the list."

"I'm honored," Beck said, and she didn't say it just to feed the author's ego. She actually was honored.

Marcia Graybill wasn't the only one to call Beck. She heard from both Lenora Palmer and Janie Foster, who called to tell her they had seen the news coverage and wanted to thank her for finding the person who had killed their friend. Janie Foster, in particular, was thankful to know that not only was Peggy's murderer now behind bars, but also the person who had killed her friends, the Bakers. Lenora Palmer insisted that Beck visit her again to tell her the whole story. She asked Beck to bring along her grandmother and sister, too. She promised to take them to lunch, go shopping, and give them a tour of the city—the whole Palm Beach treatment. Grammy and Lizzie were thrilled.

All three of the O'Rourke women had been interviewed again by Devon and other officers, as well as some FBI agents who had been searching for Edward Baker, Jr., for quite a while.

And Devon stopped by a couple of times, unofficially, just to have a cup of coffee and visit. Beck wasn't sure who was more pleased about that—her or Grammy.

He seemed to be taking all the publicity very well about three civilian women capturing the killer after the police arrested the wrong man. He did mention more than once, though, that if Beck and her grandmother had told him that Teddy was at the book signing, he probably would have figured it out for himself. But Beck was pleased to see that he wasn't one of those men who got too defensive about being beaten at his own game.

On his latest visit, Beck walked him out of the bookstore after he'd spent a half-hour having coffee and Danish with them.

"You know," he told her, when they reached the door, "back in college, when we had that class together, I thought about asking you out."

Beck laughed out loud. "I don't believe that for a second."

"No, really, I did."

"Well, why didn't you then?"

He put his hands in front of his face in mock protection. "I was too worried about my grade point average."

She swatted his arm in jest. "Would you get outta here? Go do your job."

He stepped outside but stopped on the porch and stared at her intently. "Seriously, though, maybe sometime …"

Beck's eyes twinkled, and she gave him an amused smile. "Maybe," she said. "Sometime." Then she gently pushed the door shut.

Leaning back on the door, Beck hugged herself, closed her eyes, and an expression of joy spread across her face.

Her sister's voice broke the silence.

"I told you men like a challenge."

Beck's eyes popped open, and she grinned at her sister.

It felt good to be a challenge.

About the Author

Judy Moore is the author of the popular thriller, *The Mother-in-Law*, as well as three traditional mystery novels: *Somebody in the Neighborhood, Murder in Vail,* and *Murder at the Country Club*. Her newest work is a cozy mystery, *A Book Signing To Die For*, the first in a series set in the Beach Reads bookstore in Manatee Beach, Florida. She has a master's degree in journalism from the University of Florida and worked as a newspaper reporter, magazine feature writer, and publications editor for several years. A former tennis pro, Ms. Moore's writing background also includes sports writing, and athletes from various sports are sprinkled throughout some of her novels. A lifelong resident of Florida, she currently resides in Vero Beach.

Excerpt from
Somebody in the Neighborhood

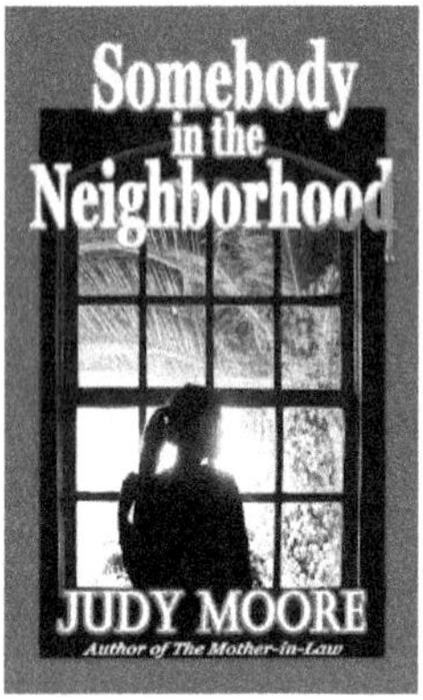

Somebody in the Neighborhood is an earlier mystery novel set in the same town of Manatee Beach, Florida. It is the story of the mysterious murders on the beach alluded to in this book. Though not in the same Beach Reads series as A Book Signing to Die For, some local characters appear in both books.

Dawn Andersen and her parents are horrified when her carefree Aunt Amy is found stabbed to death on the beach, the second woman to be murdered in the small oceanside town of Manatee Beach. The police have arrested a homeless man for the murders, but is he the real killer? Dawn, 25, makes the biggest decision of her life when she decides to leave her routine existence in Ohio to move into her aunt's cottage a block from the ocean. As Dawn learns more about her aunt's life in Florida, she becomes convinced that the murderer is closer than she ever imagined, that her aunt's killer is actually somebody in the neighborhood.

Chapter One

Dawn prodded, pushed, and cajoled her mother to show her the photograph. She had to see it—she couldn't explain why.

Finally, she succeeded, and immediately wished she hadn't.

Her aunt's body lay face down in the sand, her blonde hair so clotted with blood that you couldn't tell what color it was. She wore a pair of khaki shorts and a long-sleeved white t-shirt that were a mass of punctures, sand, and dried blood. Her arms were outstretched, her fingers digging into the sand, as if she were trying to crawl away. One of her sandals had fallen off, and a strand of seaweed wrapped around her bare foot.

Dawn had quickly looked away, wishing she could erase from her brain the awful last image of her beautiful aunt. She'd tried ever since not to think of that horrible scene on the beach, but her mind kept going there.

They learned right away that her aunt's death wasn't the first one at night on the beach. Three months earlier, a young cashier at a nearby grocery store also was found clubbed on the head and stabbed multiple times. The newspaper said she had been known to jog on the beach at night. The police were focusing on a group of homeless men who lived in an encampment behind some sand dunes in a mangrove nearby, but there hadn't been any arrests yet.

Dawn loved her Aunt Amy dearly, though she hadn't seen her in two years, not since her aunt moved to South Florida. Amy was her mother's younger sister, her only sibling, and was actually closer to Dawn's age than to her mother's. So, they'd always been close. Amy was a free-spirit, a flower child from a new generation, who had enchanted Dawn for as long as she could remember. Amy took Dawn to her first rock concert—a reunion tour of The Moody Blues—showed her how to make love beads and feather earrings, and taught her how to create beautiful batik prints and colorful tie-dye shirts.

Dawn's mother Betsy and her Aunt Amy were so different that sometimes Dawn couldn't believe they were actually sisters. Amy had a gypsy soul, never worried about anything, and saw the best in everyone. Dawn's mother, on the other hand, was usually one big ball of stress, hyper concerned about every detail of her life—and Dawn's—and always expecting the worst. The sisters had a strong bond though, an unbreakable bond, or so it had always seemed. But something happened between them, some kind of falling out, and Amy suddenly moved a thousand miles away with only a brief goodbye and no explanation. Dawn kept in touch through emails, texts, and Christmas and birthday cards, but the responses from her aunt were brief, and she hadn't been back to Ohio to visit. Dawn's mother refused to talk about it, absolutely refused, no matter how much Dawn questioned her. And when she asked her father, he'd become uncomfortable and immediately direct her back to her mother.

Her parents had flown immediately to South Florida to identify the body and talk to the police. But they had trouble getting any information from them. The police just kept saying the case was under investigation, and wouldn't give any details. It was so frustrating. Her parents also made a cursory visit to Amy's house looking for paperwork they would need to settle her estate—bills, insurance policies, tax information, and other documents—to take back to Ohio with them. Search as they might, though, they couldn't find a will. So, Amy died intestate, with everything going to her closest relative, Dawn's mother, Betsy Andersen.

Dawn's father drove Amy's Volkswagen Beetle back to Ohio, and Dawn picked up her mother at the airport. Somehow, her mother had managed to keep her grief under control in Florida, but the moment she got back to Columbus, she absolutely crumbled.

Though devastated herself, Dawn pushed her own sorrow aside to comfort her mother, who had immediately gone to bed, and didn't get out of it for four days. Dawn thought she might have to be checked into some kind of facility. She feared her aunt's death had sent her mother's fraught nerves over the edge because she knew her mother's pain came not only from her sister's death, but from the guilt she felt over their argument.

"Whoever thought there wouldn't be time to patch it up?" Dawn heard her mother say more than once to her father.

When her mother finally emerged from her bedroom, she sat at the dining room table staring in a daze at the stack of papers that represented what was left of her sister's life. She complained over and over again about how much easier everything would have been if Amy had left her estate in better order.

"She just turned forty, for God's sake! That's the age when you should be thinking about things like wills! But, no, not Amy. Not carefree, irresponsible Amy."

Then a tide of crimson would slowly creep up her neck and envelop her face, the shame for criticizing her poor dead sister totally overwhelming her. She would burst into tears again. "What was she doing out on the beach at night? Didn't she know how dangerous that could be?"

Dawn was suffering too. She'd never experienced the unexpected death of someone so close to her. It seemed unreal—she found it difficult to believe it had actually happened. It felt like someone had punched her in the stomach so hard that she couldn't catch her breath. And then the numbness set in. She couldn't sleep, couldn't eat, and sometimes found herself sitting on her couch staring at nothing, in a daze, with no idea of how long she'd been sitting there. She barely left her apartment except to check on her mother and drag herself to work, a place she found hard enough to go to under normal circumstances. During this ordeal, just being there felt unbearable.

When the time came to go back to Florida to decide what to do with Amy's house and possessions, Dawn asked if she could go along. She missed her aunt, missed her vibe that had always struck such a chord with Dawn. She felt an overpowering need to be in Amy's space, to absorb her energy, to feel close to her.

Dawn also had another reason for wanting to go to Florida. She had decided she might want to move there. A real estate agent told her parents the housing market in the area was a little slow at the moment, but was likely to take off in a year or two. They would be smart to rent the house for a couple of years, he'd told them, rather than selling it now. When Dawn heard that, the idea of moving to Florida had planted itself in her head. During the weeks that followed, the idea grew into an obsession.

She wanted to see the town and the house where her aunt had lived. Her parents owned it now, and they might agree to let her live there. Of course, she never would have considered moving into Amy's house if she'd been murdered there. That would have been impossible. But since her aunt had been killed down the beach, nearly a mile away from her house, it didn't seem so morbid. Or frightening.

Dawn was anxious to see what life could be like for her in Florida. She wanted to escape the northern winters, her dull routine, and most of all, her job. She didn't know how much longer she could bear working for her boss, Rondell Carpenter, the man who leaned in too close to give her instructions with his cigarette-tinged breath, who pushed himself against the back of her chair and put his hands on her shoulders as he read off her computer screen, who backed her into a corner twice while she made copies in the Xerox room. He reeked of aftershave lotion that she could still smell for hours after he left the room.

"Call me Ronnie" the married father of three teenagers told her every time she called him Mr. Carpenter. She never did, but she stopped calling him Mr. Carpenter, too. She tried not to use his name at all.

Lately, he had started massaging her shoulders as he stood behind her critiquing her work on the computer screen. His hands on her felt—grotesque—that was the only word she could think of to describe it. She'd squirm uncomfortably trying to release herself from his grip and had even gotten up and left her chair a few times, making a lame excuse that she needed to get something from the supply closet. She asked him to stop once, telling him she couldn't type when he did that, but the look he gave her told her she had offended him. He was her boss, she needed her job, she needed the salary to live, and he knew it.

Dawn wanted to report him to someone, but he was president of the mid-size printing company where she worked as a graphic artist. She didn't know who to go to—they didn't have a human resources office—and she wasn't sure what she would say. He was always invading her space, but he'd never actually done anything blatant enough that she would categorize as sexual harassment. She didn't know if the shoulder massaging qualified. She definitely felt, though, that it was only a matter of time until it escalated.

And to make matters worse, other employees were giving her the cold shoulder. She could tell they were gossiping about the extra attention the boss was giving her. Who knows, maybe they thought something was going on between them. Could they possibly think that? Disgusting! She didn't have anyone to confide in at the company, to ask their opinion on what she should do. She'd only made one real friend at work in the two years she'd been there, but she'd moved away a few months before, and Dawn hadn't really bonded with any of the other employees.

Besides her slimy boss, she loved her job, and really loved the work. So, lately, she'd learned to just keep her eyes on her computer screen and concentrate on the designs she enjoyed creating so much. Most were for corporate annual reports, brochures, and flyers, and some were for election campaigns. They also produced a lot of publications for Ohio State, for many of its different colleges and sports teams. She was gaining so much valuable experience, but she was beginning to think, at what cost?

For the first time in a while, she wished she and Luke were still together. He was so level-headed. He would have given her good advice. He would have been sensible and caring and listened to her. The problem was, he was a little too sensible, too passionless, and too staid for her tastes. The shelf life of their relationship had run its course in less than two years.

And she couldn't tell her parents. God no! Who knew what they would do? Her mother would probably march down to the office and tell him off in front of the other employees. Just what she needed. And her father, well her father would force her to quit. But she didn't want to do that. Amy was the person she wished she could talk to. Amy would have had good advice for her. If only she could have talked to Amy.

Her boss wasn't happy about her taking time off to go to Florida, but she didn't care. If she had her way, it wouldn't be long before she'd be kissing that job goodbye.

CPSIA information can be obtained
at www.ICGtesting.com
Printed in the USA
LVHW041552020920
664876LV00014B/1827

9 798647 475152